M000303892

KNUTE ROCKNE
THE FOUR
WINNERS

THE HEAD, THE HANDS, THE FOOT, THE BALL

Originally published in 1925.

©2004 Universal Values Media.

Republished by **Once and Future Books** (Falls Church, Virgina), an imprint of Universal Values Media. All rights reserved. No part of this edition may be reproduced, stored in a retrieval system, or transmitted, in any form, or by any means, electronic, mechanical, photocopying, recording or otherwise, without the prior written permission of Universal Values Media.

ISBN 0-9729821-0-8.

To Arnold McInerny

Member of the Notre Dame football team.

Killed in action at Chateau-Thierry, July, 1918.

A man whose loyalty to his school, to his friends and his country, whose gentlemanly conduct, scholarly attitude, courage and conviction, and high sense of honor make him an ideal of which Notre Dame is justly proud.

CHAPTER

1

HOPES AGLIMMER

There was a hushed tenseness in the air as the last of the boys finished tying their shoelaces or buckling their belts. The Springfield High School squad was going out to scrimmage for the last time before the big game; today the coach was to make the final cut and decide the personnel for the trip. There were still forty men out and the coach had announced that after this scrimmage he would cut until only twenty-five remained. It was a crucial moment.

Resolution and determination were in every gesture of Elmer Higgins as he adjusted his thigh pads; there was a set grimness about his mouth as he tightened his head-piece lacing. The year previous had been his first on the squad and he had rather expected to be cut early on account of lack of experience. This year, however, he had survived the early cut and had played for a minute or two in one of the first practice games. He had a feeling that his opportunity had not arrived as yet, but this afternoon he was determined that he would catch the eye of the coach and that when the train pulled out for Hillsdale he, Elmer Higgins, would be a member of the squad sitting with swelling chest in the coach while the cheering section of the student body down at the railroad station gave their last "nine rahs for the team, Team, TEAM."

Out on the field a few minutes later the coach lined his players up in three teams; but Elmer was not among them. He was one of the few left over and was to be used as a replacement man later in the scrimmage. With enthusiasm undimmed, however, Elmer sat on the sidelines giving no thought to the scrimmage but with his mind going over what particular plays he would use should he be called on to go in there and run one of the teams from the quarterback position. Once in a while, it is true, his thoughts strayed back to the scrimmage, and hazily he could see Hunk Hughes, dynamic halfback of the regulars, go slicing off tackle and now and then catapulting right over the line itself. After one of the pile plays there was a call for the doctor and the quarterback of the team scrimmaging the regulars was assisted from the field, limping, with a badly sprained ankle. Then, at last, loud and clear, came the vitriolic voice of the coach calling,

"Higgins, Higgins! hurry up and get in here."

Elmer felt that his great hour had come. He took off his sweat shirt in a short count and before he knew it was out on the field playing safety on defense. Three and four yards at a crash the regulars were still eating up the ground towards the goal line! Suddenly, on an apparent off-tackle play, Hunk Hughes reversed his field and came tearing towards Elmer with all his 185 pounds of bone and sinew. Elmer waited until he was just within striking distance. Then he drove at Hughes with every ounce of energy his mere 135 pounds could muster, his arms swinging wildly to wrap the on-coming flyer. There was a dull thud and Elmer knew no more until his eyes opened and he found himself lying on the rubbing table in the lockers. There was no one with him but old Doc Dixon, the local physician who always donated his services to the high school team. Doc smiled.

"Well, you've come to, Elmer. You're all right. You just got a slight concussion from meeting one of Hunk Hughes' knees head-on. He's an awfully hard man for a little fellow like you to tackle from the front. But never mind, you're all right. I'd just suggest that you go home and go to bed early and don't eat any dinner, and tomorrow you'll feel as fit as ever."

Still feeling a bit dizzy Elmer made his way into the showers, took his bath, and was out again and almost completely dressed before the rest of the squad came in from the field. The first string squad stripped and hurried to the showers from which the noise of their rough play and their singing easily reached Elmer's ears. When

Hunk Hughes, stripped save for a towel, came along Elmer could not help but admire his wonderful physique. Powerful legs, slender waist, deep chest, massive shoulders, this young giant had all the life and spring of a cat and withal a facial expression that denoted bulldog courage and fearlessness.

"Tough luck, boy," said Hunk pausing for a second, "I'm sorry I hurt you."

"Oh, that's all right," Elmer replied, "it's all in the game. I should have had more sense than to try to tackle head-on a player of your power and ability."

Hunk continued on his way, the expression of his face showing he was not displeased with Elmer's honest compliment.

Many thoughts flashed through Elmer's mind as he sat there, still a little done up, waiting for the all-important list to be posted. Why did he always get such breaks? None of the other quarterbacks could have done any better than he had done if forced to tackle the redoubtable Hunk out in the open all by themselves. Why didn't he get a chance to run the team on offense so that he could show the coach some of the uncanny generalship, some of the choice plays based on a straight analysis of conditions that he was perfecting in his own mind? He would have used these plays in such sequence that the coach would have found that Maddocks, the left tackle, was weak against plays to the inside while the big right tackle, Mac, though a terror on close plays, was weak against plays to his outside. Both of these men had a tendency to play out of position and Elmer felt sure he could have easily shown the coach these points by gaining ground against their weaknesses. Besides helping the team as a whole, this also would have helped him in securing that recognition which he felt was his due because of this knowledge of the game, based on close observation and study. Well, he might still have a chance; the coach might have at least admired the courageous way in which he unflinchingly dove at Hunk; his name might still be on the list when it appeared. He hadn't given up hope yet, by any means.

Just at this moment in stepped the coach himself, a bull-dozing, swaggering sort of fellow who had no respect for the points of view or rights of others and who got results mostly by ruthlessly driving the young charges under him. Fear was the one thing he implanted, and a shiver ran down Elmer's back as he saw that the eye of the coach had caught him.

"You may look very pretty in a squad picture, young man," the coach sang out sarcastically, "but it takes guts to play this game, you know, and I'm afraid you haven't got it."

Elmer winced. Was it courage, was it nerve, the coach meant?

"Furthermore," the harsh, rasping voice went on, "you are too small. This is a game of bone and muscle. It was never got up for little fellows like you. Turn in your suit tonight and be sure there's nothing missing."

So the blow had come! Dull, listlessly, and with lead in heart and feet, Elmer made his way homeward that evening. Gone was the fire of nervous energy which had warmed his entire being all that fall. All the ambitions of his stout heart and clean mind were crumpled; he felt down and out and all the more so since he dreaded meeting his father after such a failure. His father had warned him against playing football and had told him it was a game only for boys with strong backs and weak minds. He had told his father that he was wrong, that the game was one requiring brains, and, braggart-like, he had even said that he himself was the "brains" that was going to make the Springfield High School team feared throughout the state. And now here he was, — dropped, finished, done for! His bitterness of heart was all the deeper because he felt that he had been dropped without cause, without having been given even a fair chance. What would his father say?

His father who conducted a modest law practice in the town was already home when Elmer got there. Glumly, and without a word, the boy ate his dinner, then helped his mother clear the dishes off the table. He told her of his misfortune easily enough; it was never hard to tell his mother anything. And the kindly sympathy she gave him was an opiate to his frayed and high strung nerves. She understood. She always did. But his father —

When, finally, he went into the living room and hesitatingly told old Mr. Higgins what had happened his father gave him a brisk answer.

"That's fine," he said. "Now your career is all in front of you and it won't be cluttered up by any funny notions about playing football. If you had made the team I had made up my mind not to send you to college. Now, however, I intend you shall go to my old school, Dulac University, and study law under my old friend, Professor Noon. I have had some correspondence with him about it already and he has kindly offered to get a job for you sweeping in the law building; that will pay part of your expenses; I'll take care of the rest. Your grandfather before you was a lawyer who never had the benefit of a college education. I worked my way through Dulac University and I intend that you shall have the same opportunity."

"But Dad," the now thoroughly downcast Elmer replied, apparently not at all enthused over the prospect of going to college, "won't I be able to go out for the Varsity football team at Dulac?"

Mr. Higgins took off his glasses and while he wiped them with his handkerchief appeared deep in thought.

"Well," he said finally, "if you can't make the little Springfield High School squad on account of your size I guess you won't last long at Dulac. But I presume you'll be more satisfied if you go out there and wear one of their suits a few afternoons, so, all right. But don't forget, you're going to Dulac to learn to be a lawyer, not a pugilist, and if some big fellow there happens to smack you like Abner Hughes' boy did this afternoon don't write home to me for sympathy."

Late the following Saturday afternoon news came over the wire that Springfield High had triumphed over little Hillsdale by a margin of one touchdown. Down at the corner drugstore there were rumors of some great ball carrying by Hunk Hughes, playing that had more than offset a clever passing attack of Hillsdale's which at times had threatened to sweep Springfield off its feet. Hunk had proven himself more than a team and in the second half the heavy and powerful Springfield squad had worn out the light Hillsdale line and in the last quarter had swept their way through for the winning touchdown.

There was joy and sorrow in Elmer's heart at the news. There was

joy for the school, and the team, and there was joy for Hunk, because
he liked Hunk, — he was a good sport. There was sorrow, too, because of the credit everyone would now give Coach Smith for this
victory. In his heart of hearts Elmer felt that Coach Smith was not a
good coach but merely lucky in having on the squad such a great boy
as Hunk Hughes as well as others of almost equal ability.

Elmer took little interest in the rest of the season even though
Springfield won all its games and in a post-season contest captured
the championship of the state from the big metropolitan team which
had heretofore been unbeatable. He didn't attend the banquet given
by the Kiwanis Club and the other citizens of Springfield in honor
of the championship team and Coach Smith. His father who was a
Kiwanian urgently invited him to attend but Elmer didn't feel in
his heart that he could enjoy it; he just pleaded a sick headache as
his excuse, — and stayed home.

The rest of the winter he spent in hard study. But his studies
were not confined to his school books. He read with avidity all the
technical books written on football by college coaches that he could
lay hands on, and at night spent hours with pencil and paper dia-
gramming strategic maneuvers to be used at critical moments in
imaginary games. He played them out on the paper in every imag-
inable detail but of course from a purely hypothetical point of view.
Come what might he couldn't give up football altogether.

That winter Elmer and Hunk Hughes became very fast friends
and when Hunk told him that next fall he was going to State University Elmer did his best to try to talk Hunk out of that idea telling
him all the superior benefits to be derived from four years at Dulac.
Old Abner Hughes was a State man, however, and Hunk told Elmer
that if State was good enough for his Dad it was good enough for
Hunk, and furthermore that State, now in a period of athletic de-
pression, needed someone to bring their team up where it would
once more be the pride of State's alumni. So the two boys chummed
it together, victor and vanquished, big fellow and little, in school
and out, the burden of their common interest and most of their
talk being football. Whichever way they would go, together or sepa-
rately, their hearts were one in their love for the great game.

The following summer Elmer got a position driving a laundry truck in town. In the early twilight of the evenings he would spend hour after hour throwing passes in the vacant lot to some of the younger boys who lived in the neighborhood. Hunk, who also lived nearby, came over occasionally and did some punting with him. He was always tactful and sympathetic in criticizing some of the technique in Elmer's method of throwing the ball and always ready to praise him but all the time he honestly felt that Elmer could never "make it." He was too small, too light.

"Don't be too disappointed if you don't stay on the squad your Freshman year," he said one evening. "It's just possible, you know, that you're a little too small for college football."

And so "little Elmer," little only in his short stature and light 135 pounds made ready for his college career.

CHAPTER

2

"FRESHIE"

Dulac University was quite different from what Elmer had expected. He was surprised to find such a beautiful campus and felt a tingle of enthusiasm at the thought of spending four years among these ivy-covered buildings, under this canopy of beautiful elms and maple trees which lined the walks running around the rectangle and sheltered the various buildings. The whole atmosphere of the place seemed to be one of enthusiastic activity, alive with the hailing voices, the greetings and handshaking of the upper classmen who had not seen each other during the summer. Everybody hailed everybody else and it seemed to Elmer as though the very sight of the college men walking around the campus gave him a friendly entree to the big fraternity of Dulac men.

There was talk in the various groups about class leaders and social activities and the schedule of classes; and there was the usual lining up for places to eat and the securing of living rooms in the dormitories. There were also serious discussions as to "How about the team?" Everybody seemed worried about the rumor that Captain Lefty Latham might not return. Wouldn't Coach Brown have a terrible time trying to fill his place if such a rumor became a reality?

Elmer's nerves were all alive, — would the time ever come when the campus gossipers would worry whether or not he would return some fall? That would be sop enough to satisfy the vanity of anybody. And, by George, he was going to surprise the wiseacres back in Springfield and his kind father, too, but most of all he was going to surprise the man for whom he cherished a keen dislike, — Coach Smith of the home high school.

The tedious details of registering being over, Elmer found somewhat to his disgust that the first year of study in his law course would be entirely what was called Pre-Law; that is, English, Latin, Philosophy, History and Politics. He had hoped to get away from the monotony of this sort of curriculum and to jump right into the study of law itself. However, he was told that he would have to spend one year at Pre-Law before taking up the technical subjects themselves. He was also listed for Physical Training but was told that if he made the Freshman football squad he would be excused from Physical Training during that period.

"When will the call for the Freshman squad come out?" he inquired of his next door neighbor after they had started an acquaintanceship by bumping into each other in the process of getting their trunks into their rooms. But his next door neighbor knew even less about Dulac affairs than Elmer knew and was plainly in the same state of bewilderment.

That evening, his first day complete with a full schedule of classes, Elmer picked up the college daily and there in the headlines was the announcement that the Varsity football squad was to report for equipment on the fourteenth so as to start practice on the fifteenth. He thrilled even at the sight of these momentous words. Then, in the announcement a little lower on the page in type not so heavy, he found instructions that highly interested him. All Freshman candidates were to report at the gymnasium on the fifteenth for equipment so as to be ready for practice on the sixteenth. The time set was three o'clock and Elmer began at once to arrange his plans so as to be sure to be there on the dot. He immediately saw Professor Noon, his father's friend, about his work and the kindly professor took him in hand and showed him what rooms were to be swept out every day. As Elmer's classes lasted until three o'clock and as he confided in the professor his ambition to go out for the Freshman football team he received permission to do his work after dinner every night and he was told that his task would not occupy more than an hour every evening. Elmer went to bed that night with a feeling that his life at Dulac had really begun.

The scene on the fifteenth was an exciting one for Elmer. At three o'clock near the head of the line of a group of some hundred boys there he was awaiting his turn to receive equipment. There was considerable jostling and pushing but the assistant Varsity coach in charge kept matters in good order, assuring the boys that there was plenty of outfitting for everyone and telling them that they must take their time and their turn.

"High school days are over now, you know, fellows," he reminded them. "You're college men now."

Elmer received an unwelcome surprise when he discovered that the equipment handed to him must have been worn by some Dulac Varsity man a century or more ago; the stockings and jersey had holes in them; the pants were too long; the shoes were not of a kind particularly conducive to speed. Elmer started to protest and to point toward some new pants in the corner but the upper classman in charge of the supplies scarcely noticed him, dryly remarking for the benefit of all:

"Take what you get and be glad. Freshmen don't get much around here except abuse."

Of course that silenced Elmer's protests. He was more satisfied when he noticed that the other Freshmen were all similarly equipped in old castoff suits, though he thought to himself that if he were in charge of equipping, those men who had enough ambition and energy to go out for the team would be treated with a little more courtesy and favor.

Next afternoon about the same hour Barry, the Freshman coach, called the rookies together. He gave them a sound man-to-man talk every word of which Elmer took in seriously, though he could not help smiling to himself when the coach told them that above all they must forget everything they ever learned on the high school gridiron because "whatever football you learned there was wrong."

"Smith of Springfield," said Elmer to himself, "I wish you could be here for this." However, he thought the statement a bit sweeping and rather unfair to men who coached high school teams like Hillsdale, for he had heard it said more than once that Hillsdale was as well coached as most college teams.

"Also," the coach went on, "I don't want any fellow out there to think he is better than anybody else. Football consists primarily of tackling and blocking and nobody can make this team if all he can do is carry the ball, forward pass or punt.

"If a man can do these things he must be willing to go out and do the unselfish, mediocre work of blocking and tackling; these are the backbone of the game. If there are any of you spoiled high school stars here who don't want to learn how to block and tackle turn in your suits tonight; you can't make the team here. Furthermore, I want only men out here who can think; if there are any among you who are rattle-brained, or a little dull mentally you'd better get over it or get out. We can't use that sort. We can use only those who come out here with a clear mind and with a mind which can concentrate on a subject with some sign of durability, say for an hour or two anyhow."

The coach paused to let that sink in; the Freshmen all looked self-conscious and for a fleeting second Elmer felt as if he were himself the dullest fellow that had ever breathed.

"And there's another thing," the coach continued giving the young greenhorns another shock, "you Freshmen aren't going to get an awful lot of coaching this fall. You'll be too busy acting as shock absorbers for the Varsity. You'll be allowed two games away from home but these games will be merely incidental; your big job will be to scrimmage the Varsity, not only on defense, but to learn each week the plays of the particular team which the Varsity plays the following Saturday and to scrimmage against the regulars for all you are worth.

"There won't be any glory in it this fall, — nothing but hard work, abuse and grief." He paused again. "However," he went on, "those men who do their job well this fall will be awarded by Coach Brown on my recommendation, a numeral jersey. Besides that, you will have had the satisfaction of having done a man's work well and of having helped to better prepare yourselves to try out for the Varsity in your Sophomore year."

The entire squad of more than one hundred men was now cut

up into small groups and first put through some setting-up exercises before practicing the stunts of falling on and picking up the ball. The man in charge gave a clear cut picture of how the thing should be done and often his remarks to the men as they tried to fulfill his instructions, unsuccessfully, were sharp and sarcastic, Elmer coming in for his full share of this sort of verbal discipline.

"Fall around the ball, not on it! Keep your eye on the ball; don't be afraid to leave your feet. You must be married and worrying about your wife and family the way you save yourself!

"Bend down and pick up the ball like athletes; don't pick it up like an old man ninety years old. Bend at the knees and waist. You're not doing a one-step with a flapper!"

After half an hour of this kind of work the squad was again divided; the linemen were taken over to one side and shown the various stances of the positions. But Elmer, with all the others who had declared themselves backfield candidates, was put into another group, and this, in turn, divided into backfields, received two simple plays to run off. The skeleton team in each group consisted of the backfield and the center only. The two plays were fullback through guard and halfback inside of tackle. They ran these plays until Elmer, for one, was sick and tired of them; but just then the head Freshman coach lined them all up, asked for volunteers to punt, and set them at taking turns going down the field covering these kicks. That was some relief but at 5:30 the Freshmen were all glad to make their way back to the Gym.

That evening Elmer dropped in next door to see his neighbor. Joe Ruggles was his name; he came from a large city in another state.

"I don't think much of this Freshman-Varsity football out here," he told Elmer. "Looks to me as though we are going to take a lot of beatings and I don't think we are going to learn very much."

"Well, I don't know," said Elmer, "I don't care particularly how much we do learn; the only thing I am concerned about is whether or not all of us will get a chance. There are a hundred of us out there and there isn't anybody any smaller than I am."

Ruggles, a strapping fellow of 180 pounds, good naturedly smiled.

"Well, I guess when they cut they won't cut out a boy of my size. But I've heard this that Head Coach Brown of the varsity is looking for brains and I guess if you can show him brains you'll get along all right."

"I hope so," Elmer answered; but he wasn't very hopeful. "The trouble is Coach Brown won't pay much attention to the Freshmen. It looks to me as though our staying or not staying on the Freshman squad will be entirely up to Mr. Barry. He's going to handle the Freshman team this fall and the point I'm interested in is, will Barry have time in sorting over these hundred men to look for brains? If they go through the same stunts they did in high school simply picking those fellows who look the best physically, and who hit the dummy harder, I don't believe I'll get any more chance here than I did back at Springfield." He then confided to Joe his experiences on the Springfield High squad, and the bitterness of heart he experienced at the hands of Coach Smith. He also told him of his hopes and ambitions and of the amount of time he had put into studying strategy, and modestly remarked that he thought he could forward pass as well as the average freshman in college. Joe Ruggles was very sympathetic and it was evident that Elmer and he were going to become fast friends. The two boys, by their antithetical natures, complemented each other; Ruggles admiring the high strung, fiery, nervous disposition of Elmer while Elmer admired the genial, good natured, happy-go-lucky disposition of big Joe.

The next afternoon the Freshmen were assembled at 3:30 and they were all sent down covering kicks for a little while. Barry, the Freshman coach, then ordered everyone down to the tackling dummy. Here they were shown how to tackle a dummy both from the front and from the side. And here, too, the particular points about "leg drive, eyes open, head back, and meeting the dummy squarely with the shoulder" were all enumerated. The dummy was very hard and after each tackle each player had the sand from the pit running down the innermost recesses of his suit, making every one of the boys feel decidedly uncomfortable.

After an hour of this work they were lined up again in skeleton backfields and given three more plays which they were told were plays which had been used the previous year by Kingston, the first big eleven the Varsity was to meet that fall.

The rest of the week and the first of the following week was spent in rudimentary and fundamental work. The following Wednesday Coach Barry began scrimmage between the various Freshman teams so as to enable him to make his cuts and pick the men who were to scrimmage the Varsity the following Saturday. Wednesday, Thursday and Friday afternoons as these Freshman elevens scrimmaged up and down the field they looked to Elmer like so many mobs. Some knew their signals and some didn't. Some knew their assignments, but most of them didn't. There was no attempt made to use any tactics in strategy; it was merely a matter of calling a play regardless of position or down, and trusting to luck that it might go. The team Elmer ran on Friday had two backs who seemed to know their positions fairly well but the third, a right halfback named Durley, seemed to have no idea what it was all about. As a result Elmer kept calling the play in which Durley carried the ball and Durley made some big gains while the rest of the team did some fairly good interfering and blocking.

To Elmer's intense surprise, when the list was posted that night, giving the names of the thirty-six Freshmen to remain on the Freshman-Varsity squad, he found that of the eleven men who were scrimmaging with him only his name and that of Durley remained on the list. Feeling a certain sense of elation as he wended his way back to the dormitory with Ruggles he could not, however, help but voice his dissatisfaction with the unfairness of Freshman Coach Barry giving credit to the man Durley who carried the ball because there was nothing else he could do out there.

"It looks to me," remarked Elmer to Ruggles, who was now nicknamed "Rip" because of the slashing way he played guard on defense, "as though we have another one of those master minds coaching our Freshman team. Here he goes and gives me credit for good judgment in using my best back Durley on the weak point of the other team, when as a matter of fact it was the only play that would work because Durley simply didn't know what to do or how to do anything when he wasn't carrying the ball. It was the only thing I could do if we hoped to gain any ground and the other two backs who ran such splendid interference out there had their work entirely overlooked."

"Well," Ruggles answered, "they can get a lot of experience playing on one of the intramural teams this fall, and if they have any stuff in them they'll have plenty of chance to show it next spring when the head coach gets them out for spring football."

Saturday's classes at Dulac were over at noon. On the following Saturday after lunch Rip, Elmer and several of their classmen sat up in Elmer's room and discussed the coming scrimmage with the Varsity.

"It's a good thing Lefty Latham got back today," said one of the Freshmen ends.

"Why?" asked Ruggles.

"Well, one of the fellows overheard one of the Varsity coaches say that they had nobody at all to fill his place at center."

"Yes," said another, "and they say Lefty Latham has been one half the line by himself for the last two seasons; it certainly is a big boost for the Varsity to get him back again. They lost four of last year's regulars by graduation."

"Well, even with Lefty Latham out of there," said a third freshman, "I dread to think of the scrimmage this afternoon; the Varsity will surely give us a terrible going over. They'll all be out there trying to make a showing in front of the coaches; they're figuring on that Kingston trip. If anybody thinks this is going to be a tea party I'm afraid he's going to be sadly mistaken."

"Those Kingston plays look pretty good to me," said Elmer, "and we ought to gain some ground; but shucks, what am I going to do if they put me in charge of a team with Durley at halfback? We won't be able to do anything unless I give Durley the ball continually."

"If I were you," said Rip, "I'd give the other fellows the ball and then the coach will see Durley's a poor interferer, and messes things up most of the time."

"I'll try it," said Elmer, "but I'm afraid the coach will put all the blame on the ball carrier and probably won't even notice that Durley isn't taking out his end."

CHAPTER
3
SCRIMMAGE

The scrimmage that afternoon proved the most exciting experience Elmer had as yet had at Dulac. The first string Varsity was able to score just once against the first Freshman team opposing them, Rip Ruggles doing some beautiful bull work in the defensive Freshman line, stopping play after play at different parts of the field, plays which aimed at two or three positions from where he was playing. Elmer got in with the third string Freshmen team, late in the afternoon, against the third string Varsity; and sure enough, just as he had feared, Durley was assigned to right halfback on his team. On the few occasions on which the Freshmen got the ball Elmer called on Credon at left half to carry it, and on each occasion Credon was thrown for a loss or no gain, because Durley proved totally incompetent in the task of handling the defensive end of the Varsity. Whenever this happened, Elmer would drop back on the fourth down, himself, in the absence of a better punter, and boot the ball down the field thirty-five yards to the Varsity. About the fourth time the Freshmen got the ball Elmer for the first time called the play in which Durley carried the ball off-tackle, and because Credon knocked the defensive right end flat on his back, Durley went for ten yards before he was down.

"That's the play you should have used long ago," said Coach Barry. "Durley seems to be about the only freshman we have that can advance the ball with any consistency. Now go ahead and continue to use him and we may be able to score on the Varsity."

Elmer was disgusted, but he obeyed and said nothing, continuing to call on Durley to carry the ball again and again, either inside or outside of tackle, and because the Freshman left end and Credon ran some fine interference, Durley invariably was able to gain ground.

On his way into the Gym after the scrimmage, Elmer felt himself boiling over when he heard Coach Barry telling one of the student reporters that the feature of the Freshman play that afternoon, besides the remarkable playing of Ruggles, was the all-around playing of Durley, right halfback.

That evening Elmer had another half hour chat with Ruggles and some other freshmen in Rip's room. Elmer vehemently gave tongue to his disgust with Coach Barry for giving the credit to Durley, who was at best just an ordinary player.

"You can figure," said Elmer, "that all the spectators would give Durley the credit, but you would think a coach, at least, would give credit where it is due."

"Oh, let's forget it, and play a round of whist," said Rip, "we haven't anybody to beat this fall anyway. The two games we have are unimportant and we'll just spend the fall out there learning a lot of football and what difference does it make who gets the credit?"

"That's all well and good," said Elmer, "but if the Varsity team is coached on the same principle, I'll be very, very much disappointed and I might even be inclined to think that my father was right."

The succeeding weeks found Durley moved up to the first string halfback on the Freshman team, while Elmer continued to fill in at third string, which meant that he got in only now and then, and always with just a makeshift outfit. However, he was learning a lot of football every time the Freshmen scrimmaged the Varsity, as the Varsity was beginning to work like a well-oiled machine and the Varsity quarterback, Shorty Dunne, was certainly nothing else but a field general.

Elmer enjoyed watching Dunne look over the Freshman team and, down after down, pick out the various weaknesses which cropped out, and go driving a play to the spot where the Freshmen least expected it. If the Freshman center got pulling out too fast, *zing!* on the next play there was a delayed line play, crashing through the Freshman center for fifteen yards. When the Freshman tackles moved in too tight Dunne went outside them, and when they widened he drove through inside of them. When one of the Freshman guards, in his enthusiasm to help the other side of the line, pulled out of his position he must have been stricken, for on the next play, as he repeated the same stunt, he found the Varsity fullback sprinting through the hole which he had just left vacant. When the Freshman fullback started going up a little too close to stop the line plunges, they completed a nice little forward pass over his head, and because the rule in football is that a team with the ball should never forward pass on the first down, Shorty Dunne threw a long forward pass for a touchdown to one of the ends who was able to get past the Freshman halfback because he apparently reasoned that no forward pass could possibly be made on the first down and came tearing in as soon as the play started. Dunne took no unnecessary chances, seemed to weigh his values carefully, and as far as Elmer could see made no mistakes.

The whole Varsity team seemed to have a mental poise so fine and so disconcerting to the Freshmen, that in the third week the resistance to the Varsity had dropped to a low ebb.

"We can't stop these fellows," said one of the Freshmen halfbacks, "they know too much."

"They sure do," Elmer chimed in. "If your shoulders are set for one thing they certainly will always give you the other thing. What we ought to do is to be alert for everything and not commit ourselves to any one thing."

"Yes," said the halfback, "but Coach Barry stands behind us and hollers, 'look out for a forward pass,' and when we drop back the Varsity pulls an end run on us and Barry instead of taking the blame himself puts it on us."

The night before the team left to play the first big game at Kingston was the occasion for a tremendous rally around the big bonfire on the Varsity field. It was Elmer's first real taste of Dulac spirit in full action.

Coach Brown and his assistants sat up on the stage with the entire team and some old grads who had returned especially for this forensic feast. The entire student body and several members of the faculty were gathered in the stands close in front. The band played "Alma Mater" and the students gave all the yells with such a gusto that Elmer, yelling with the rest, felt his veins tingle. The head of the student board then stepped on the platform and introduced the various speakers.

The first speaker was the chairman of the faculty board, a dignified old professor, who remarked about the thrills he always got on an occasion of this sort, and on the fact that he felt confident the Dulac boys would uphold all the fine traditions of sportsmanship, courage and fair play that had always characterized Dulac teams. He paid tribute to the boys on the team, said they were above the average as students and praised them as gentlemen and as representatives of Dulac.

The next speaker was a wealthy alumnus from Chicago, a prominent attorney, who took the crowd through twenty years of the history of football at Dulac, starting back with the days of the famous Red Fish and bringing his memoirs up to the present. This old grad made a great hit with the boys, particularly when he implored them to be sure to wallop Kingston because his law partner was a Kingston man and he asserted there would be no living or working with him if Kingston won. His remarks made Elmer think of his Dad at home, himself a Dulac man who had never lost the spirit of the old school.

The third speaker was an assistant coach who was extremely bashful and whose few remarks were simply to the effect that he was very glad to be back helping to get the team ready for another year.

Freshman Coach Barry, Elmer's chief, then spoke. He was proud, he said, of the part he and the Freshmen squad had played in developing the Varsity and some of the upper classmen started a round of applause at that. "More Dulac spirit," Elmer said to himself with a thrill.

Head Coach Brown of the Varsity was then introduced. He confined himself to a few words regarding the strength of Kingston and the weakness of Dulac, his remarks being received with a good deal of appreciative laughter. Kingston's, he said, was a very good team; but Dulac's was a team of fighters; and the game wouldn't be over until the final whistle was heard. He got a cheer on that.

The final speaker was Lefty Latham, Varsity captain and center, whose appearance was awaited with a tense interest as this was probably the first public speech of his lifetime. Lefty arose very much flustered. He floundered around with a few remarks about not having any team if it wasn't for the student body and then, in his nervousness, becoming just a little incoherent he said:

"If you students do your part then I'll do the best we can."

Which simple announcement was received with the loudest spontaneous yell that Elmer had ever heard in all his young life.

The entire meeting was one of thrills and enthusiasm and as the gathering arose at the finish, and, accompanied by the band, sang the "Victory March" of old Dulac, Elmer felt his very heart swell with the spirit of loyalty and determination to give his best forever and forever, to make "Dulac win, — forever and forever."

The Freshmen squad received a few days rest while the Varsity was away. Saturday afternoon all the stay-at-homes went downtown to get the returns of the game with Kingston. Dulac's victory is now a matter of history but there were probably no prouder men, even on the Varsity itself, than Elmer and Rip that night as they walked back to school and recounted to one another their good fortune in being part of such an institution, and in particular a part of the athletic organization which had so many noble traditions, traditions which they were now daily living up to. The two boys felt lifted up with a reverence and enthusiasm for Dulac.

Every day that fall was chuck full of memorable incidents for Elmer but probably the greatest event insofar as he was concerned, was when he got into play the last quarter of a game against a neighboring Normal school. The Freshmen were hopelessly outclassed by the heavy Normal team, and Coach Barry, evidently foreseeing that there was no chance to win, put in all the players available and among these was Elmer. He went on to the field with every nerve "pointed" and with all the energy of his being set to turn the tide. But it was too late. The Normal team finally rolled up a score of 42-0 against the battered and discouraged Dulac Freshmen.

The college paper reporting the game the next morning carried a statement quoting Barry to the effect that the Freshmen had been too badly battered in their scrimmages with the Varsity to do themselves justice, and declared that if these boys were to play Normal again they would have no trouble beating that team which was described in the article as "not much good at its best."

Whatever respect Elmer had had for Coach Barry was dissipated when he read these alibis.

"If Coach Barry had picked a few interferers and put them on our team instead of all ball carriers we might have been able to do something," he said to Rip at lunch that day. Not only Rip, but every man who heard the remark agreed with him. It was plainly to be seen that Elmer Higgins was learning football the one and only way it can be rightly learned, scientifically, by the head.

In the last week of the season the Varsity did nothing but light work and the Freshman squad was dismissed for the year, everyone of the men who competed in the game against Normal being awarded a jersey with a class numeral on it. Elmer felt mighty proud of his class numeral; but he felt sorry for Credon, one of the left halfbacks who had had the misfortune all year to be teamed with Durley and had not had a chance to get into the Normal game because, from Coach Barry's point of view he was not good enough. Elmer was frank in speaking about this to Credon several evenings later when he chanced to meet him on the quadrangle, but Credon seemed to honestly think he really wasn't much good and that the coach was right.

"A coach is a coach, you know," he said. "He does the thinking."

"Yes," Elmer answered, "but no football team would ever win if the players themselves didn't think, too." There was not a grain of the mutinous or rebellious in him, but he hated to see a man like Credon discounted by the mistakes of others.

All the Freshmen football men joined the track squad during December but Elmer's thoughts were mostly on his studies and on going home for Christmas. His letters home were full of that now. He didn't say much about football. Early in the fall he had, of course, written to his Dad that he had made the Freshmen team but his father's response had been a little dampening.

"The Freshman class this year at Dulac must be a little under par," he had written, "and the Freshman football team in particular must be having an off year." This nettled Elmer for a minute but then it amused him for his satisfaction at having made the team was too great to be spoiled by his Dad's dry comment. He knew his Dad!

For the first month or so Elmer had also exchanged letters with Dora Spaulding, a home girl for whom he had had a sort of fancy since first they were thrown together during their high school days. But Dora had not answered his last two letters, so Elmer had taken a particular satisfaction in writing her again, telling her he had made the Freshman-Varsity team. At the same time he told himself that girls didn't amount to much anyhow; they only distracted one's thoughts from one's career. But even if Elmer had regretted the break-off in correspondence he was far too busy to give it any thought.

Elmer spent a very enjoyable vacation over the holidays with the folks back in Springfield and did quite a bit of strutting with his numeral jersey along with Hunk Hughes who had been the star of the Freshman team at State. Chumming it once more with Hunk, he was having a perfectly happy time in spite of certain gossip going around the drugstore to the effect that Dulac must have been short of Freshman quarterbacks if little Elmer Higgins could win a numeral. This remark was said to have been made by Coach Smith, who was still coaching Springfield High. It caused Elmer only to bite his lips, clench his fists and swear to himself that he would yet show the town what a big dub this home coach was.

Elmer's mother, of course, was sympathetic and frankly proud of her boy's achievements. From Mr. Higgins, however, there were at first no comments whatsoever on football; he confined his conversation about Dulac to inquiries about Professor Noon and some of the other faculty members who had been there in his day. But one day he did ask Elmer if he should not feel satisfied, now that he had made his Freshman numeral, — warning him against getting any false notions about going out for the Varsity team. To this Elmer only responded that he meant to go out in the spring for exercise anyway if for nothing else; and there the subject was dropped between them. In his heart, nevertheless, Elmer knew he was going out there determined to give his right arm, if necessary, to achieve his goal.

Returning to school after the holidays Elmer settled down with Rip to plug and study hard for the midyear examinations which were coming on soon. A few days after school reopened Coach Brown called a special meeting of the Freshman football squad and talked to the players for the first time. His remarks were short and to the point.

"I don't care how fine a football player any of you boys may be," he said, "you are no good to the school or to me if you don't keep up in your classes. You might just as well be over playing with Kingston or South Square, our two biggest rivals, as to be going to school here if you are not keeping up in your work. So, if you are up, stay up; if you are down, get up."

CHAPTER

SPRING PRACTICE

In the last week of February the mid-year examination marks came out and several of the most promising Freshmen were sent home for flunking according to rumors Elmer heard around the campus. He and Rip had passed, however, with flying colors though he had a close call in Latin. Naturally he was elated; and the results of his up-and-coming scholastic work were quickly evident on the athletic field. In an open novice track meet held a day or two after the exams Elmer surprised many, including himself, by winning the quarter mile in what was considered fairly good time. The Gym record in the quarter was fifty-two seconds; Elmer negotiated the distance in fifty-four and one-fifth seconds.

The Varsity track coach, old Dad Moore as he was called, was enthusiastic and wanted Elmer to drop everything else in athletics and become a runner. Elmer, however, told Dad that running didn't interest him nearly as much as playing football and that he was expecting Coach Brown to give the call for spring practice as the snow was practically all off the ground. Dad appeared greatly disappointed.

"You may make the Varsity football team, even if you are a little small," he said, "but you would make one of the greatest runners Dulac ever had; that is if you put your heart into it. If you don't make the team next fall will you promise me you will come out and work with the track team from then on?"

Elmer promised; but he felt fairly confident that Dad would never have a chance to call his bluff.

On the last day of February Coach Brown issued his call for all candidates for spring football which was to be for all freshmen interested in making the team, and for all upper classmen who in their hours of recreation were not busy with some other Varsity sport. More than a hundred men answered the call and were equipped that afternoon. The notice also carried the announcement that there would be a forty-five minute blackboard trial every evening after dinner in the Science lecture room. Elmer set his thoughts forward for all this with the keenest anticipation.

Coach Brown was not out for practice the first afternoon scheduled and not much was done, the work consisting almost entirely of informal kicking and passing around the field. That night after dinner, however, Coach Brown addressed the boys in the Science lecture room and outlined the series of talks he was to give over a period of six weeks at the end of which he would give a written examination that he might check up on those who knew football by that time and those who didn't.

"The first thing I am looking for this spring," the coach said, "is brains. Of course you must have a little physique, and you must develop speed, and when the scrimmage comes you must show that you have what we call intestinal fortitude.

"However, there is always a scarcity of brains, and as football today is largely a contest of wits I want men who have them and who can use them. A lot of you big fellows here probably think that because you weigh around two hundred pounds that you'll make the Varsity in a canter next fall. You may, but you won't do it on weight alone, not by a long shot. If any of you are suffering from charley horse between the ears you won't even be invited to go out next fall."

The coach then went into a discussion on the comparison that could be made between a football team and an army, between warfare and football, and Elmer found himself deeply absorbed in this. He had never had football put to him in that light before.

"The attacking team," said the coach, "may be likened to the attacking army and the defensive team to an army protecting its position. The line of scrimmage of the attack can be used either as artillery or as infantry; the quarterback is the chief of staff and all that goes with the chief of staff. The offensive backfield may be likened to the cavalry and its versatility is increased because it can, upon a signal from the chief of staff, be changed to an airplane squadron.

"On the defensive side the defensive line may also be called either infantry or artillery depending upon what kind of attack it is called upon to meet. The defensive backs may also be cavalrymen, bayonet men, or anti-aircraft men depending upon the style of attack the offensive is using. If the offense tries to run the ends, the line is the artillery which breaks up the formation; and the secondary backs are cavalry who then come up and knock down the man carrying the ball.

"If the offense tries a line buck or a mass play the defensive line is again the artillery which breaks up the formation, and as the lone carrier of the ball comes through he is picked off by the defensive backfield men who, in this case, may be said to be bayonet men.

"In case the offensive team tries a forward pass the defensive team is like the infantry trying to capture the grounds where the hangars are before the airplanes can leave the ground; while the defensive backs are anti-aircraft men who try to prevent the airplanes from destroying their basic connections which is the same as completing a forward pass.

"The commissary departments of both teams are the water boys; the secretary of war of each army is the head coach; while the President and his cabinet can be likened to the chairman of the Board of Control and the faculty and alumni who make up this personnel.

"And yet," Coach Brown went on "although the tactics and strategy involved in football are, in a certain sense, similar to those used in warfare there are some serious differences between warfare and the game of football. Warfare is a serious thing in which the lives of thousands of brave men and the safe defense of a country are involved. An army, therefore, can not afford to take any chances. The men who control its destiny must at all times be careful not to unnecessarily endanger or sacrifice human life. They must keep the army intact for the defense of their country.

"Football on the other hand is just a game. In case one of the opposing teams scores a touchdown there is nothing much lost. There is no irreparable injury done. There is nothing to prevent the other team from coming along later and scoring two touchdowns. In warfare if a man's life is lost irreparable injury is done, and if an entire army is destroyed, with it may be lost the liberty of a nation. In football, however, which, as I say is just a game, the two teams can take all kinds of chances. I don't mean by this unnecessary chances, but chances in which, if the maneuver works well, a game that has been apparently lost may be won. In other words, a touchdown may be merely a means of spurring the other team to greater efforts so they can still come back and win the game.

"Now, while I insist that you boys all play football as I coach it, I don't want you to get the idea that this is the only way to play football. There are a dozen other good ways of playing it. This, however, is the only way I know, and as far as we are concerned it is the best way. And yet as far as outsiders are concerned, other ways may be just as good and we must recognize this for we have no room here for the egotism of the know-all sort.

"I intend to show you how we do everything in football, and I intend to give you in each and every case a good reason why. There is no such thing as the last word in football. New angles to the game are cropping out continually, if any of you men have any ideas which are new don't be afraid to express them. Only the jackass knows it all and brays; and only the donkey keeps still and lives without ideas. Be here tomorrow night at the same time and bring notebooks along prepared to take notes as we cover the subject."

On the way back to the room Elmer and Rip discussed the talk and agreed that if Coach Brown practiced what he preached they would both be on the squad next fall, although Elmer expressed himself as being a little dubious, feeling that Coach Brown had been, in a measure any way, expressing himself along these lines for effect on the faculty.

"Well, we'll see," said Rip. "The spring practice will soon tell us."

On the field spring football proved to be a drill in fundamentals; a lot of work was done in passing and catching passes, punting and catching punts. The assistant coaches, including some of the seniors who were to be graduated that June, had charge of most of the detail work and plugged hard trying to perfect individual players in personal proficiency in handling the ball. Coach Brown had Rip Ruggles over with the head line coach getting special instructions in line play, and for the first few weeks he seemed to ignore entirely the existence of Elmer as well as a few other Freshmen. On this account Elmer began to feel even more skeptical than ever and was going over in his mind different schemes for trying to get recognition from the man in charge. He knew what he wanted and he knew what he could do; but it was a tough job getting anyone else to see it.

After lecturing about a month Coach Brown began asking hypothetical questions of various players in the class which still numbered more than seventy men, very few having dropped out. Right through a long list of queries Coach Brown kept after his student players for their opinions. Whenever one was stumped it was always Elmer who raised his hand and in most cases answered the question. To his surprise he noticed the rest of the class began to show an intense dislike of him for this reason. Even Rip remarked on it.

"I believe I'd keep that right hand down for a while, Elmer," he said. "The rest of the brothers are beginning to get a bit jealous."

"Let them get jealous," Elmer answered. "I'm determined to get recognition from Coach Brown by any fair means, and by foul means, too, if necessary." And Rip could not help but laugh at the grim seriousness of the flashy-eyed, diminutive lad whose whole being seemed to spell personality whenever he discussed football.

"Foul means?" Rip repeated. "Oh, no, not you, Higgy."

"Well, you know what I mean," Elmer answered cooling down. "I'm going to let him know that I'm at Dulac this year."

On a Saturday night in the middle of April the Freshman class had its big social function of the year, a reception to the faculty followed by an informal dance. Elmer didn't know any girls in town, but Rip Ruggles, who had on several occasions stepped forth into the social whirl of the town of Dulac, volunteered to furnish a charming partner for the evening. Elmer was loath to accept the proffer but Rip finally persuaded him that he ought to go, — it was his duty as a college man to try to enjoy as many activities as possible. And so Elmer went.

The reception was held in the University gymnasium. Shortly after Elmer ran the gauntlet of the large receiving line of the faculty members and their wives, the orchestra struck up the first dance number. The young lady Rip had brought along as a dancing partner for Elmer proved to be a quiet, demure maiden who didn't rasp on Elmer's nerves as some of the other girls present would have done. Elmer had no trouble filling his program and didn't pay much attention to those with whom the dances were exchanged. For his third dance, however, as he was looking around wondering who his partner was to be, a tall, lively-eyed slender girl left a crowd of students and came over to him.

"I guess this is our dance," she announced. Elmer collected himself and their dance began.

They swung around the room to the rhythm of the orchestra for a short time in silence and then the young lady suddenly asked:

"Aren't you the young man everybody is calling Shorty Dunne, Jr., another master mind of football?"

Elmer felt a surge of blood to his head and knew that he must be presenting the appearance of a blonde, sunburnt in the tropics. He strove for speech but he couldn't articulate. Finally his sense of humor came to his rescue and he laughed with his partner as he retorted:

"You can go back and tell some of those young lollypoppers who prompted you to ask me this question that at least I have a little courage and am no quitter. The only quitters we have around here at Dulac are the fellows who never try anything but merely sit around and criticize."

The young lady laughed uproariously at this but Elmer could see nothing particularly funny in it and after the dance he sat over in the corner and watched his erstwhile partner make her report to the group. He spent the rest of the evening in rather surly silence, which must, no doubt, have greatly puzzled Estelle Wilson the girl whom Rip had brought for him. He mentioned the incident to Rip between dances but got no sympathy from him for Rip also thought it was a good joke and had a hearty laugh over it.

Elmer took his young lady home in a cab, maintaining a moody silence, and was scarcely more than polite in his departure when they arrived at the Wilson home. He was none too happy over his first Dulac social function and was beginning to feel that some of the fellows, at least, decidedly had it in for him.

Several nights after the dance as Coach Brown was closing his football class he asked the following question:

"What would you do with first down, ten, on your own fifteen yard line, the score nothing to nothing, ten minutes left to play before the end of the game, — there is scarcely any wind but your punter is no better than the punter on the other team, and the other team presents a fairly normal defense when you line up in punt formation?"

Credon, Freshman halfback, suggested a punt and so did most of the others who were asked. One or two suggested a wide end run, mostly for position to punt on the ensuing down. There was a pause and then Elmer raised his hand.

"Well, young man," said Coach Brown, "what's on your mind?"

"I want to answer that question," said Elmer. "I believe that by this time I would have found which of the three defensive backs was weak against the forward pass, and if I found this man was a defensive man backing up the line I'd shoot my two ends away down the field as decoys. I would have the man back there in the back position in punt formation, and fake a punt, and throw a forward pass to the quarterback straight up the middle of the field. If the man back of the line is weak on passes he will get by him, but the pass must not be thrown so long as to go down deep into the middle of the field where the last man on defense is waiting to receive the punt. It must be a fairly long pass but not too long."

There was a touch of amusement on the coach's face as he listened to Elmer's answer, but as the bell rang then, marking the time for study hour in the dormitories he made no comment. "We will continue this tomorrow," was all he said; and of course Elmer was disappointed. Another chance gone! If only Coach Brown had said he was right.

Just before noon the next day Rip Ruggles came bursting into Elmer's room.

"Have you heard the news?" he fairly shouted.

"No," said Elmer. "What is it? Is the whole campus joshing me because of that answer of mine last night?"

"Josh nothing," said Rip, "the whole campus is carrying the story that Coach Brown made the remark to Dad Moore that spring practice had been a distinct success, — that he had found the thing he had been looking for — brains! And the brains in the person of one Elmer Higgins. Congratulations, old boy, aren't you just tickled to death?"

That noon at the Commons where they ate Elmer noticed a changed look of respect with which the other students eyed him, and at the same time a certain feeling of satisfaction took hold of him as he felt that at last he had aroused the coveted attention of his chief and had passed through those stages of ridicule and grief through which every young fellow has to go before he arrives.

Spring football closed a week later with a final scrimmage in which Elmer played first string quarterback against a picked Varsity squad and while he didn't show anything brilliant, he made no mistakes and as far as any comment by the coaches was concerned there were no particular criticisms of his work.

There was no publicity in the papers because no one was paying much attention to the position of quarterback in spring football, — the great Shorty Dunne still had another year. This pleased Elmer as he dreaded publicity. He spent the rest of the spring in studying and taking in an occasional social affair; but his whole being was more or less enthused with the prospect of studying next fall under Coach Brown and the quarterback of quarterbacks, Shorty Dunne!

CHAPTER
5

LEARNING FROM COACH AND LIFE

Several weeks before the close of school Dad Moore met Elmer on the campus and asked him if he had time to drop over to his room for a little chat. Elmer went at once to the old man's quarters in the gymnasium, a modest, well-furnished room, the walls of which were covered with pictures of track stars running and jumping, besides certain medals which had been left there by some of his old-time performers. Dad was an old bachelor, a man whose life had been devoted to developing young men physically; besides being track coach he was also trainer of the football team.

"Well, young man, I guess you are lost as far as track athletics are concerned," said Moore giving Elmer a chair. "The old man thinks pretty well of you as a prospective quarterback in a year or two; in fact I think he is counting on you to take Shorty Dunne's place when he graduates."

Elmer blushed and modestly mumbled something.

"What I called you over for, however," Dad went on, "was to see if I could get you to act as one of my camp counselors up at my summer camp in Wisconsin." Dad Moore then went on to explain that every summer he had a camp for boys up in Wisconsin, and that he always took along four or five Dulac boys as counselors. There was no salary, just the payment of all expenses. But the camp offered a glorious summer vacation and at the same time the development that comes with shouldering certain responsibilities; for each of the eight boys in a group was directly under a counselor and each counselor was responsible for the life and limb of every one of the boys under him.

Elmer was delighted with the opportunity and said he would write home for permission at once. The reply from his Dad a few days later was in the affirmative, although he mentioned the fact that Elmer's mother was disappointed in a way but readily gave her consent because she realized that it was for Elmer a golden opportunity. Elmer carried his father's answer back joyously to Dad Moore and received from him the plans and arrangements for the camp. There was to be a meeting in Chicago, a farewell dinner there to all the parents, and then all the boys of the camp, the counselors, and men in charge were to leave on a special train for the Wisconsin woods. These plans being all settled Elmer felt a load lifted off his mind for the question of what he was to do during the summer had already worried him.

A week before the examinations in June Coach Brown called a meeting of all the candidates for the fall and gave a long talk on what he expected of the men during the summer.

"I don't want anybody to go out and work himself so hard he'll come back here all worn out and underweight. Neither do I think it's a good thing for any of you young fellows to sit behind a steering gear all summer or suffer sore ankles from the sharp turns on the dance floor.

"If you do these things you'll come back here so out of shape we never will get you in trim for football this fall. Rather, I expect a sort of halfway policy. Wherever possible I want you to go and take a rugged out-of-door job; do a certain amount of hard work; and above all, you fellows who are working your way through school, save all the money you can. Come back to school in fair shape, rugged, brown, and healthy, so that when practice opens on the fifteenth we won't have to waste too much time on conditioning but can start learning right away."

After the meeting Coach Brown walked with Elmer over to his room and said he wanted to go in and have a chat with him. After inquiring of Elmer how he was doing in his classes and what he had in mind for the summer, the coach went on to say there was something on his mind that they ought to talk over; and Elmer could not help but feel impressed with his chief's friendly and unostentatious manner.

"I hope you haven't got any exaggerated idea of yourself or your ability just because you happened to give some good answers in class this spring, or because you wrote such a fine examination paper on football," Coach Brown began. "I'm rather sorry that my complimentary remarks about you got out so much because with some young men it might not have been taken as it should. Some coaches like to drive and abuse their squad continually. That may be all right but I don't believe in doing it. I realize that you fellows are all young boys and that you are entitled to a little word of praise now and then as a reward for good work."

Elmer was silent but he felt his heart glow toward the "big chief" as he spoke these words.

"However," the coach continued, "you fellows on the Freshman squad have a long way to go. None of you are anywhere near the stage at which you might be called 'nifty.' Some of this year's Freshmen are still so clumsy that whenever they cross the field they sprain their ankles in imaginary holes. But they have their good points. They are a clean, wholesome bunch of boys who come from good families. They have a world of enthusiasm and I believe they are impressed with the many school traditions here to which they will have to live up.

"They have been executing a lot of details this spring rather crudely but constant repetition of these details will finally produce results, so that they will become part of their reflexes, and when all the correct ways of doing things become part of a man's reflexes then, and only then, does he become a great player.

"Now that is what I want to impress upon you, Elmer." The coach drew some papers from his pocket "I'm going to leave with you a copy of the plays for next fall, all diagramed out with the signals for each one and I want you to practice playing hypothetical games with these plays all summer against six or seven defenses which I am also giving you on paper. If you do this and do it faithfully, by next fall when you are playing quarterback, the instant you have analyzed a defense, the right play will suggest itself and you can adjust your choice of plays as dictated by the tactical situation.

"The question of downs, number of yards to gain, position on the field, direction of the wind, the score, and time left to play must, of course, be ever present in the mind of every man on the team, but particularly in your mind, the mind of the quarterback. I know you'll be happy and busy with Dad Moore up there in the woods but you ought to systematize your day so that after the boys are all asleep, if you take just one hour a night to do these things you'll be surprised next fall at the way you will have developed."

Elmer gave Coach Brown his promise to adhere to this scheme and to guard as sacred the plays and signals which had been given him. When the coach left him that night he was an excited, yet deeply and solemnly impressed young man. The thrill and joy of football had long been his, but now, for the first time, an abiding sense of responsibility on the team came to him and filled his mind.

The morning of the last day of school was filled with hustle and bustle. The street cars and cabs going to town were loaded with students and their suitcases, while truck after truck went down the beautiful elm tree drive laden with trunks for the depot. There were hurried goodbyes and admonitions not to fail to write as the jolly groups broke up and went on their various ways for the summer vacation. The seniors, of course, stayed over for the commencement exercises.

As the street car sped down the road the last sight of the school that Elmer had was a clear view of the Law Building which he had swept all year and which housed his good friend, kindly old Professor Noon. Now, however, his thoughts were coming one after another, too fast for reflection on any one thing. He only knew that his first year at Dulac was ended and that his first football dream had come true. He was a happy lad.

Things went fast from that moment of leaving school. Two days at home with his parents; a minute or two with Hunk Hughes and the crowd down at the drugstore; and before he knew it he was on his way to Chicago. There was a banquet there at the LaSalle Hotel, a jolly mixed gathering of boys going to camp, their parents, the camp leaders; another scene of hurried good-byes, and the train pulled out for Wisconsin.

The site of the camp was delightful, set up on a well-wooded spot on the shores of a lake which proved to be stored with many kinds of fish. The whole atmosphere of the place was exhilarating and Elmer felt that he was to enjoy himself to the utmost in spite of the fact that he had the responsibility of eight boys directly under his supervision. He found time in the evenings for work on his hypothetical football, though often he found it a trying task to follow up those studies, for the doings of the day were always strenuous and there was no time, as far as the group leaders were concerned, for reveries. The job of keeping the boys happy, contented and busy was an exacting one.

There was only one incident that was outstanding during the summer, and that happened while Elmer's group was away on a three-day canoe trip, up one river, across a portage and down another. The second stream proved to have a remarkably fast current and when the boys began to insist on going in swimming Elmer held back his consent for a while on account of a natural prudence. However, the youngsters were so enthusiastic, so determined he finally gave in; and so in they all went, their leader with them.

The spot they had chosen was a beautiful, sheltered place where the current didn't prove too swift. In a little while Elmer relaxed his vigilance and made his way down stream a few rods around a bend. There, on swimming out to mid-stream once or twice he found no difficulty in getting back to the dead tree limb which hung low over the water.

"I'll call the boys to come here," he was saying to himself. At that moment while he was hanging on the limb, resting, he was suddenly startled by cries from the boys around the bend, above stream, and next saw in the water a dark object floating towards him. He recognized it instantly to be a human being. He was galvanized into action. He let himself down, reaching out as the object floated by, and, grasping it with one hand, hung to the branch with the other. His grip was firm but his heart seemed to stop beating as he recognized the unconscious figure to be one of the boys of his group.

Calling for help to the other boys who by this time were running towards him he got the young lad quickly ashore; they resuscitated him in a short while.

The boy said he knew nothing except that he had suddenly grown weak and didn't remember what happened immediately afterwards. None of the other boys had noticed him losing control of himself. It had all happened so swiftly that he had been caught by the current before they had cried their alarm.

Lying awake that night Elmer found it hard to go to sleep. This brief, terrifying experience continued working on his mind. Perspiration broke out on him as he thought of the consequences had he not been fortunately hanging to the tree limb, right in the path of the current when the boy's body had come sweeping along. It brought home his responsibilities with a multiple effect, and on the remainder of the trip he "played safe," with relentless caution, vowing to himself that never again would he relax his vigilance in any way wherever he might be. How often Coach Brown had told him and his companions in their football lectures about "eternal vigilance." Now, he felt, he knew what these words meant.

The camp broke up the last week in August and Elmer hurried home to spend a week with his folks before returning to Dulac.

On his return to Springfield he found the whole town agog over the news that Coach Smith had been appointed head coach at State during the summer. The preseason dope on football, as Elmer found, was going full blast at the corner drugstore. He met Hunk Hughes who had spent the summer in Spring field and he heard many things of the liveliest interest to him, he had been so out of touch with things all summer. Among other things mentioned was a rumor that Dulac and State might resume athletic relations in the near future. Elmer got a real thrill out of that.

"We would surely like to play you," said Hunk. "I think we're going to have a great team at State this year and with Coach Smith taking hold of us I don't think State will be the doormat it has been for the last few years."

Elmer said nothing but he thought a great deal. "Coach Smith!" he commented to himself, and there was scorn in the thought. He had learned much already about what real coaching is, from his chief at Dulac.

Mr. and Mrs. Higgins could see a big change in Elmer, — their little boy was decidedly growing up. There was a new air of dignity and responsibility about him and it was evident that he was taking life and its problems more seriously than ever before while he was in a certain sense still just a boy he was immeasurably more mature. The year had wrought many changes and apparently all of them for the better. But of course nothing was said about all of this; the parents kept their thoughts to themselves, and Elmer's father in fact, continued to treat him in his usual gruff, half-teasing way.

When Elmer suggested that the folks come down to Dulac for the big game of the season with Aksarben all Mr. Higgins would say was that he never saw a game of football in his life and he was too old to see one now. However, when Mrs. Higgins saw how disappointed Elmer was at this she confided before he left for school, that his father had whispered to her that both of them might be down for the game after all.

And so Elmer went back to school that September a happy fellow. Before he realized it he was on the train on his way back to Dulac; and once on it he could hardly wait for it to get there. The pleasurable anticipation of meeting his college friends again was surprising to him. He hadn't known that he cared so much about them. They had all grumbled a bit the previous year about this, that and the other thing, and he didn't realize, until he had been away just how much the old school meant to him. Now he would begin his regular study of law and in this one prospect alone he was intensely interested.

And there was football! Since his conversation with Hunk regarding the possible State game in another year he found that his interest was doubled, trebled! How he would like to play against a team coached by Smith! If he ever got into a game like that he knew he would surprise Smith; in fact he would even surprise himself.

A game with State — and he on the Dulac team! The possibility seemed almost too good to be true.

CHAPTER
6

LEARNING AT EVERY TURN

I sure am glad the coach has promoted you to the second team," said Rip to Elmer, as they sat together in their room about a week after the opening of school. It was the evening of the day on which this new stride in Elmer's advance took place.

"Yes, and it makes me feel pretty good," replied Elmer. "I only hope now that Shorty Dunne doesn't get hurt. I'd like to have a season to study under him before undertaking any such responsibilities as the running of the team in a big game."

"Well," Rip went on, "Shorty is a rugged boy, and can take a lot of punishment. But we fellows that were freshmen last year have a lot of confidence in you.

"Thanks," said Elmer, "that makes me feel real good, Rip. But the rest of the backfield are all seniors, and I don't believe they'd feel any too sure about me if I were to get out there in some big game and start calling numbers."

The roommates resumed their studying at this point; but through Elmer's mind ran various ideas as to what he could do to inspire confidence in himself among the older heads on the team. After he went to bed that evening, he lay awake for hours, running over in his mind various ways and means to achieve his ends. As yet, he had no chance to realize his possibilities, or his limitations; he had as yet, himself, no tangible evidence as to what he really could do. He had hopes some day of being a Shorty Dunne; and yet of late certain fears had beset him that perhaps his old archenemy, Coach Smith, was right; that he was no good; that he never would be a football player. Which would he realize, his hopes or his fears? His last thoughts before he dropped off to sleep were hazily to the effect that he must, he must, he must make the team!

The first two weeks on the field were confined almost entirely to fundamentals. To Elmer's surprise, all the drudgery of blocking, tackling, and falling on the ball was gradually turned to play. The exhilaration of being actually a contender for the team changed entirely his point of view, and the things which at one time had been nothing but drudgery, were now executed with snap and enthusiasm. The coach spent most of his time in showing him how to form a pocket in catching punts; how to squat before lunging and running interference; and also how to relax when using the dive interference. They also rehearsed four simple running plays and two forward pass plays over and over again, until it seemed that even an imbecile could remember their minutest detail. They ran these plays against another team of eleven men, who were instructed to stand there like so many dummies. In this way every man learned his assignment on each of these plays thoroughly, to such a point of perfection that what had once been mere mental reactions were beginning to develop into reflex actions.

The squad was kept in a good humor by the clumsy and comical efforts of a boy by the name of Peaches, who was trying out for tackle. Peaches had the reputation of being so clumsy and of lacking coordination to such an extent that he was even said to be an unwelcome customer in self-service cafeterias. As the story went, he had broken so many dishes and upset so many trays in these places that this year he was eating in a boarding house where everything was served to him from the head of the table.

The assistant coach seemed to take keen delight in picking on Peaches. In tackling the dummy, Peaches came up and did just about as well as he could with his big feet, big hands and contorted facial expressions.

"Not very good form," said one assistant coach.

"No," said the other assistant coach, "but the man he was to tackle was so overcome with laughter at the face that Peaches made that he collapsed. You keep making that face, Peaches, and you'll stop any ball carrier with a sense of humor."

On the opening scrimmage, Peaches, who was playing tackle on the second team, was surprised to find that he himself didn't play against the other tackle. Elmer heard the assistant coach mutter under his breath, "We'll have to dissolve the shellac off this fellow's brain or it will always be impervious to any ideas"; and then out loud to Peaches he said, "The tackle on offense plays outside the defensive guard, and on defense plays off the offensive end's outside shoulder, unless the offensive end comes out too wide. Even then, always play him with hand and eye." A smile went around at that, for everyone could see from the facial expression of Peaches that he had no idea what playing a man with hand and eye meant.

On another occasion they had a terrible time with Peaches, trying to get him to leave his feet in falling on a fumbled ball.

"Why don't I leave my feet when falling on a fumble?" asked the assistant coach, who had charge of the tackles. Judging from the bewildered look on Peaches' face it was evident that he had no idea. "My reason," continued the assistant coach, "is a wife and three children."

The next time the ball was thrown out in front of him, Peaches let himself go out into space like a huge catapult, and there was a great giggle as he lit on the fumble with arms and legs spread out in the most grotesque manner. As he didn't get up at once, but lay there, Elmer ran to his assistance and found that one hand was bent under the body. It must have been severely sprained in the jolt, and it was several days before Peaches again appeared on the field.

"If I were as clumsy as he is," said Rip to Elmer one night, "I swear I'd get a job waiting over at the ice cream parlor and spend an hour a day at coordinating exercises.

"Maybe," said Elmer, "but just the same, I think Peaches has got the kind of stuff in him that means determination. He'll learn how to handle himself some day, and then look out! With that tremendous power he has, and his wonderful heart, he'll surprise everybody — you wait and see."

After two weeks of practice the coach announced his opening scrimmage, and all the players put on extra pads so as to guard against injuries. Coach Brown was a great believer in taking no unnecessary chances in practice, and Elmer was so padded up with "rubber doughnuts" that he went out on the field feeling like an ad for a rubber tire.

While the rest of the squad was warming up, Coach Brown gave the scrub quarterbacks a few minutes over in one corner of the field.

"Well, you men have had two weeks to practice calling plays loudly, clearly, and distinctly, in a way that in music we call staccato. In this scrimmage this afternoon there are just three things I want you to remember.

"First, when in doubt, punt; second, be just as chesty and egotistical as you can be in running the team, and if any of the backs or linemen start to prompt you as to what plays to call, tell them where to get off. You run the team on offense, absolutely, and if you don't — out you'll come — so quickly it will surprise you.

"Third, and most important of all, I want you to know when not to forward pass. I don't want you to forward pass in the early part of the game, when the score is even, or in your own territory. I don't want you to forward pass when you get ahead. I don't want you to pass when near the other team's goal line, as this might go for a touchback. Don't forward pass as long as your running attack is working well. Don't forward pass when the defensive team seems to be alert and looking for it. Don't forward pass unless you have a man executing the pass who has all the qualifications of an expert. In other words, take no unnecessary chances. Your instinct will tell you when the psychological moment arrives for a forward pass. Now, this is all I am going to tell you today.

"Your instructions are simple. Use them as you go along and make sure that you stay relaxed and retain your mental poise. Pay no attention to the hubbub around you. Be sure that you are clear in your mind as to just what you intend to do. Then do it, and do it decisively."

The scrimmage between the first and second teams proved to be no cozy affair. Every man out there was fighting for his position, with the result that every man went in there for all he was worth. Shorty Dunne caught a punt and ran through Elmer's team for a touchdown to the intense disgust of Coach Brown.

"The most polite crowd I ever saw in my life," the coach exclaimed. "Eleven Alphonses and Gastons! This certainly looks like a great year for Dulac."

This sarcasm had an instant effect. It spurred the second team on in such a way that from then on they played the first team nip and tuck. The halfbacks on Elmer's team were Credon, who Elmer felt was a good back because of his interference; and Durley, who he felt just as certain was an overrated dub.

Credon tried to advance the ball and found himself unable to, because Durley was just as weak in taking out an end as he had been as a freshman. Durley made several good gains because Credon had even improved as an interferer. He knocked the end flat on his back on each and every occasion, so that all Durley had to do was to follow his interference going at the secondary defense. He always gained some yardage and as he lined up he seemed to be pretty well satisfied with himself.

The second team reached the five yard line and here they were stopped twice for no gain. Peaches, who was playing at right tackle, came back and suggested to Elmer, "Shoot thirty-three over me, I know it will go." They lined up, and Elmer called the play in which Durley carried the ball off tackle.

"Signals," yelled Peaches. He came back and demanded of Elmer, "Didn't I tell you to send thirty-three over me?"

"You go on back there at right tackle," Elmer ordered, "and take care of that job and you'll be darn busy keeping those number twelve feet of yours out of everybody else's way. I'll run this team at quarterback."

He repeated the number for the off-tackle play, and running behind the fullback, Credon and Elmer, Durley dashed for the five yards and a touchdown. Credon knocked the end flat on his back, the fullback had jammed the tackle in and Elmer had cut down the secondary. Despite this, as they went back to kick off, Durley said to Elmer, "That's the boy, Elmer, keep calling my number all the time."

"It looks like we'll have to," sarcastically retorted Elmer, "so long as you don't touch the end whenever Credon's number is called. Who do you think you are, some prima donna?"

The whistle blew shortly afterward for the end of the scrimmage, and the only thing which seemed to be on Coach Brown's mind just then was the question of injuries. Finding that no one had been hurt, he expressed himself as being fairly well satisfied, but announced that he would take up the matter of criticisms of the scrimmage the following Monday.

After they had taken their shower and were dressed Elmer noticed Durley and a group of his friends in a hushed conversation over in the corner. As he went by them on his way out he paid no attention to them, but he couldn't help hearing Durley's remark, "and he's green with jealousy of the way I carried the ball."

It was evident to Elmer that unless something was done a clique feeling was liable to develop. His first impulse was to go to Coach Brown and explain the whole thing to him; but after deliberation he decided that this was not the thing to do. He would wait until Monday and hear what Coach Brown had to say. In the meantime he kept his counsel.

The entire squad met on Monday tense with eagerness for the scrimmage criticisms, for Coach Brown had a reputation for speaking frankly, and every man was keyed to expectancy for the talk. The coach opened his remarks with a word concerning team work, and the spirit of all for one, and one for all. He went on discussing the need for more speed on offense, the need for more aggressiveness on the line on defense. He took up each man on the first team individually, and commended him for his good points and then brought out his weaknesses. Despite the feet that he mentioned names it was evident that his remarks were totally impersonal. He then wound up with the question of the value of men to a team.

"We have a tradition here at Dulac," he said, "that we give credit entirely on offense to those men who run interference, to those men who perform the menial unselfish task of knocking down and out of the way the would-be tacklers of the defense. Likewise, on defense, we give entire credit to the men who can tackle and the men who can play defense against the forward pass.

"But coming back to offense we, among ourselves, on the team, and the coaching staff, do not give credit to the man who carries the ball. The man who can do nothing, except when he is carrying the ball, the man who, because of his inactivity, causes us to have only ten men on offense when he is not carrying the ball, such a man is worth practically nothing to this team.

"As to the scrimmage Saturday, I want to assure those scrubs like Credon, Higgins, and Jones at fullback, that their interference was the sort of thing a coach likes to see. I want to warn the first string backs that they had better be up on their mettle and on their toes, or any one of these three men here might take their places over night. And I also want to very urgently request that if there is anyone here who doesn't think it is necessary to run interference, he had better hand in his suit, and the sooner the better."

It was frank talk, all right, and Elmer took it all in with profit; and not without a certain amount of speculation as to what effect the coach's last words might have on a fellow like Durley. When he came out on the field that afternoon he was surprised to see Durley over in the corner with a Varsity end, and he was further surprised to see him practicing interfering.

"Well I guess he got the shock of his life this noon," said Rip to Elmer as they were loosening up.

"Yes, but from what I see over there in the corner," Elmer answered, "he may still be worth something to the team."

The following Tuesday and Wednesday Elmer scrimmaged again and found that he had made several mistakes. Once he discovered himself on fourth down so close to the side lines that the kicker kicked out of bounds before the ball had gone ten yards. On another occasion he tried to rush the ball on his own ten yard line, and the man carrying the ball fumbled and a Varsity man recovered it. As the Varsity had but ten yards to go for a touchdown, they scored quickly.

To Elmer's surprise Coach Brown said nothing to him about this out on the field; so, after some little silent debating with himself, on the way back to the gymnasium, after practice, he walked up to the coach and spoke to him, telling him about the mistakes he had made. Coach Brown paced along with him slowly until there were no other players within hearing. Then he spoke.

"Don't ever make those mistakes again. But I'd rather have you make mistakes now and profit by them, than just do the right thing accidentally in practice and make the mistakes in a big game. Another thing, Higgins, I don't want you to have yourself carrying the ball as much as you have been. I want you to have a clear head for calling the signals, and for kicking the ball high and far when called upon to punt."

Elmer was glad he had spoken. He was learning at every turn.

CHAPTER

7

"TOMORROW WE MUST WIN"

The opening game that year was against a small normal school. The Varsity began easy, running up four touchdowns in the first half, without any particular effort. Then Elmer's turn came. Between the halves Coach Brown gave him his instructions.

"I'm going to send you and your team in this second half, Higgins, and I want you to use just three plays, and one of these is a forward pass by yourself to Credon or Durley out to the side. Do you get me? I know we haven't got this play in our repertoire, but the stand is full of scouts and I want them to see this kind of forward pass, though you can rest assured that we will never try anything so foolish in a big game. The normal team has one good tackle, the big left tackle, and I want you to hit that spot all afternoon so that we can get some practice. We have all the points we want now, and all we are out for in the second half is a workout against enough opposition to enable us to correct our weak points."

Elmer's team went into the game determined to make good on this chance. But his team scored just once in the second half; and yet the coach seemed very far from dissatisfied.

"You let yourself get into the bad lands once there, Higgins," he said, when it was all over. "But it's all right; just keep in mind that you must always maneuver so as to never get too close to the sidelines when you are about to score. Also, don't forget to use your best play on your first down. as this will put you away ahead for your remaining three downs."

It was on the following Tuesday that Shorty Dunne was hurt.

That made a sensation for the campus, and the talk increased when Coach Brown announced that he was going to keep Dunne out of the next practice game, which was against a small college from a neighboring state. "Dunne out? — who then?" Of course everybody understood that he wanted to save Shorty for the big game the Saturday following against South Square; but who would he choose to replace him in the meantime? The school was agog with gossip and speculation.

That same night Coach Brown appeared at Elmer's door.

"May I have a half hour of your time?"

As Elmer gave him a chair, he couldn't help but admire this man for his strong and direct, yet modest ways.

"I know how busy you are," Brown went on, "keeping up in your classes, and I don't want to take up too much of your time. But there are a few things we must keep in mind regarding this team Saturday. They have a fine defense, but not much of an offense, and I think it will be up to you to play a kicking game and have the whole team alert for the breaks. If you find a weak spot, nurse it along, use it just once in a while, when you have to, and try to save it for the time when it will do you most good."

The coach then went on to explain the comparative strength of the half dozen plays they were using and their use in logical sequence; how the use of one play made another play strong, and he also discussed with Elmer for awhile the relative ability of the various Dulac backs on these particular plays.

From that moment, of course, Elmer knew that his work was cut out for him. But even so, the game the following Saturday proved more exciting than he or any of his team mates had expected. It was scheduled originally as merely an easy practice game, to give the coach an opportunity to pick his thirty-three men for the big trip away from home against South Square the following weekend. To his intense surprise, Elmer didn't feel at all nervous as he lined up on the kickoff.

Dulac received and carried the ball back on the return almost to midfield. Two plays failed to gain an inch of ground and Elmer dropped back and kicked out of bounds on the ten yard line, on the third down. The first quarter was practically a constant repetition of this — Dulac unable to gain, and Higgins punting the ball back to the opponents who were also unable to gain. The result was a sort of punting duel, neither with any particular advantage.

In the middle of the second quarter, however, the Alba quarterback fumbled a punt and as quick as a flash it was recovered by one of the Dulac ends on the twelve yard line. Elmer now picked on the weak spot, which he had noticed in the earlier part of the game, and gained six yards. The next play failed to gain; and on the third down Elmer threw a forward pass, which went over the goal line, incomplete, for a touchback.

The ball was brought out to the thirty yard line, but Alba was unable to gain in three downs and on the fourth down an attempted kick was partly blocked and recovered by Dulac on the fifteen yard line. Again Elmer, on first down, hit the weak spot for seven yards, and two more plunges made it first down on Alba's four yard line. On the first down he again used the weak spot at guard, but this time the play gained only one yard, making it second down and three yards to go for a touchdown. Elmer was clearly worried, and called numbers for two or three plays, changing his mind in each case, and finally he called for a split buck which gained two yards, placing the ball on the one yard line. He got up and stalled around for about a minute. He couldn't quite make up his mind just what play to call, when "bang" — the gun went off announcing the end of the half.

On his way into the field house, Elmer, feeling very much like kicking himself all over the lot, was passed up by Durley, who said nothing at first, but gave him a sneery look. That burnt up Elmer, and fire was added as he overheard Durley remark to one of the other teammates, "Wait until Coach Brown opens up on this sap quarterback between the halves — then you'll hear something good."

It was hard to be silent then; but Elmer said nothing, for the fact is he was all set for this sort of thing, realizing that he had it coming to him because of his mistakes in forward passing on the third down, and in running the team so slowly, with so short a time left to play, that he had robbed them of a touchdown.

He wondered what Coach Brown would say. But to his surprise Brown merely took him over to one side and asked him, "Do you realize now the little mistakes you made this half?"

"Yes," replied Elmer, "I'm afraid I am an awful dumbbell."

"No," said the coach, "you are getting along nicely, but of course, when near the opponents' goal, as you were the first time, I wouldn't forward pass at all. And you must always have two or three moves prepared in advance. Now, you haven't used seventy-three or sixty-eight at all, and they are primarily scoring plays to be used inside the ten yard line. So play exactly the same kind of a game you have been playing, and bear in mind not to use sixty-eight or seventy-three if your running plays are going well, but as soon as you are stopped call on them. If you happen to get worried don't show it to your teammates; always be glad and confident in appearance and near the end of the half keep in touch with the timekeeper, and *the time left to play*. In such a case as occurred this afternoon always run your team faster.'"

As Elmer went out for the second half, he felt he never could forget Coach Brown for the kindness of that criticism. "He has a heart, that man!" he exclaimed to himself; and the next moment he was onto the field, keyed up with determination to merit the coach's confidence.

The second half proved to be an entirely different game, and Dulac scored two touchdowns in short order. Shortly afterward Credon appeared on the field and replaced the left halfback. Credon reeled off some good gains and shortly after the start of the fourth quarter went over for a touchdown. Immediately after the goal was kicked, making the score twenty-one to nothing, Durley appeared, as substitute for the right halfback. What happened subsequently was a repetition of what had always happened whenever Credon and Durley were on the same team. Credon couldn't gain and Elmer became so enraged at the contemptible bearing of Durley that, when he got close to the sidelines, he called out to the coaches on the bench, "Send me out a right halfback who can interfere." However, there was no change made and they bungled along as best they could until the end of the game, the final score being twenty-one to nothing.

After the game, as Elmer emerged from the dressing rooms, he found Durley and several of his friends waiting for him.

"What a fine sneak you're turning out to be," said Durley. "Trying to make your friends look good to the coach, and make a monkey out of me, aren't you?"

With those words Durley lurched at Elmer aggressively and insultingly.

But Elmer was determined to avoid a fight at all costs. "I don't believe it's fair," he replied, "for Credon to be taking your end out for you every time your number is called, and then when his number is called to find you absolutely making no pretense of taking care of the end."

"That's none of your business," said Durley. "It seems to me Coach Brown can take care of his own job and I have a mind to give you a good licking."

Elmer's first impulse was to tie into the fellow; but he remembered Coach Brown's admonition about always bearing in mind the best interests of the team, so, still determined to avoid a fight, he merely walked away.

"I'm sorry," is all he said. "I assure you that it shan't happen again."

"You're yellow," Durley hurled at him; but Elmer made no reply, and controlling himself with difficulty went to his room.

The first part of the following week was filled with feverish activity. The South Square plays were rehearsed by the Freshmen, who used them with all the power they could mobilize against the Varsity teams, in scrimmage on Monday, Tuesday, and Wednesday. Coach Brown gave out no new plays except one trick play to be used in the latter half of the game in case they were behind, — just a play to be used as a last resort. Offensively the team had a lot of exercise, working dummy scrimmage against another Freshman team who were passive on defense, but who used the same offensive which it was expected South Square would adopt.

After practice Wednesday afternoon the list of the thirty-three men to make the South Square trip was posted. Elmer's name was on it; and so was Rip's. Rip was delighted to see his name on it, because, for some foolish reason or other, he seemed to have the idea that he might be left home. They congratulated each other and were as pleased as two young boys could possibly be. That night the students held a big rally in the gymnasium — the idea of the coach being to properly impress on the team that the student body was solidly behind them in their coming game with South Square. The entire squad of thirty-three picked men sat on the platform and listened to the admonitions of the various speakers who rose to oratorical heights in their attempt to create excitement and the proper emotional reactions. Rip was highly excited, but Elmer took everything very soberly.

"Aren't you just excited to death?" asked Rip in a pause between speeches. "Gee, I can feel the goose flesh creeping up all over me!"

"Goose flesh nothing," Elmer answered. "Oh, it's all right as long as you feel that it's helping you. As for me, all I can think of is that South Square has a veteran team. That's enough to make me realize that if I'm lucky enough to get into the game Saturday, I'll have to do some pretty tall thinking."

The last speech over and the last strains of Dulac's "Victory March" having died away, Elmer and Rip were strolling on their way back to the room, when suddenly, as they were turning up the walk which led to their dorm, they were surprised to find themselves confronted by a group of half a dozen fellows. What was this? It all became plain in an instant; for there was Durley stepping out belligerently and thrusting his face into Elmer's.

"You're the dirty sneaking hound who's responsible for my being kept off the list! Your friend Credon is on the list and my name is left off, just through your backbiting, and I'm going to whip you within an inch of your life."

"That's all well and good," said Rip quietly, stepping up. "My man can take care of himself. But I suggest that we adjourn to the gymnasium, where you fellows can put this thing on fairly and without interference."

"That suits me," said Durley, and the entire group turned and made their way back to the Gym.

Elmer said not a word. He was furious, but he was cool and determined.

Up in the boxing room both men stripped except for Gym suits. Rip appointed himself time-keeper and arranged that the combatants were to box three minute rounds with a one minute rest until one or the other gave up. Although one of Durley's friends was appointed referee, Durley didn't seem particularly pleased with these arrangements.

"Why, the little yellow stiff will quit in the first round, and I won't get a chance to get even."

"Before you get through, Durley," Rip retorted, "the only thing that will hold you here will be the four walls. You'll want to jump out of the building."

The difference in physique was only too apparent as both men advanced to the center of the boxing room; Durley was a fairly tall, long armed chap, weighing about one hundred and sixty pounds, while Elmer was of a frailer type, and weighed less than one hundred and forty. It was just as evident that if Durley knew anything at all about boxing he ought to make short work of the little quarterback.

The first round was all Durley's — a wide wild right swing landed three times on the chest, the stomach, and the side of Elmer's head; and though there was no particular power to these blows, it was evident that if this continued it would be a very short time before Durley would wear Elmer down and out.

In the intermission, however, Rip whispered to Elmer, "Every time you see that right coming in, just step inside of it, and counter with your right elbow in close."

And the advice proved perfect. Adopting these tactics in the second round, Elmer was surprised to find that Durley was powerless to hurt him, for Durley's hand was all right — his left was no good at all. The third, fourth, and fifth rounds went on; both boys were tiring fast; they were unable to hit each other. In the sixth round, Durley began to weaken disastrously, and Elmer, whose trim condition was to his advantage, began to assume the upper hand. Towards the end of the round, Durley was so tired he could hardly raise his arms.

"What do you say we call this enough?" said Durley, at the end of the round.

"No," said Rip, "my man is going to beat you to a pulp."

"No, I'm not," broke in Elmer. "If he's satisfied, I certainly am."

So the fight ended.

It was obvious, however, from the look in Durley's eye as he and Elmer undressed and took their shower, that he was far from satisfied. Mortified by their failure, Durley and his friends left.

"I'm afraid I made a mistake," Elmer said to Rip when they were alone.

"Mistake how?"

"Why, in any way to have taken it on myself to say whether or not Durley did his part. But I've seen so much injustice in that direction that I just couldn't help it."

"I don't blame you one bit," said Rip. "I never could stomach Durley or his friends, anyway, and I'd just as soon have them for enemies as not."

"Yes; but harmony, Rip — there's got to be harmony on the team," Elmer protested.

"As far as the harmony on the team is concerned," Rip came back, "we're all with you. Durley and his friends aren't on the squad and no matter what you do, he and his kind will spend the rest of the fall knocking you, and Coach Brown, and the rest of the team. You just wait and see. And don't forget what Professor Noon said, 'A man is known by the enemies he has.' So let's go home and forget it!"

The next day at noon the team left for South Square. There was no one at the station to see them off, as classes were in session. The players had an entire Pullman car to themselves. Once settled in the train, Coach Brown called the men together in groups, according to their position, and quizzed them on their various assignments, both offensive and defensive. He called the quarterbacks over to him last. Then, after the routine quizzing, came a real surprise.

"Higgins," said the coach, "I intend to start you with the second team, and I hope you can go in there and hold off South Square for a quarter. Your instructions are simple. Kick continually on third down. On first and second down I want you to try thirty-three and twenty-one. I'll have Shorty Dunne with me on the sidelines, and I want to see South Square's defense and how they meet these two plays. This will give us the key to the entire defensive situation, and will let you, Shorty, go out there having clearly in your mind exactly what to do."

The next morning found them riding along the picturesque Hudson, where the beautiful scenery of Catskills and Palisades was a revelation to all the boys who had never been East. Next came the excitement of getting the New York papers which all contained stories on the game, reporting that the South Square team had just had their last scrimmage, were in good condition, and were expected to win easily. As Elmer glanced around at the various boys who had read these articles, it appeared evident to him that whoever the publicity man was for South Square, he had used the wrong psychological tactics; for now the Dulac boys seemed more determined than ever that South Square would not win — not by a long shot!

The welcome by the South Square authorities was very cordial, and every courtesy and convenience was shown the boys in making them comfortable in their quarters for the night. Dulac was given the field for a workout between three and four in the afternoon, and there was no would-be spectator within a mile of the field. That evening, the entire South Square student body marched in a torchlight parade to the hotel where Dulac was quartered, and after giving their own yell and a yell for Dulac they called for speeches by Coach Brown, the captain, and Shorty Dunne. It was a great ovation, and in a way, strangely enough, it rather unsteadied the chaps from Dulac.

Coach Brown, however, called a meeting just before they went to bed, getting them all together in a large room.

"Some of you fellows may feel a little bit unstrung over this reception here tonight," he said, "but I want you to bear in mind that the game tomorrow means everything to us, and good fellows as they are we've got to beat them. This cheering was all right, but don't let it bother you. It's just a lot of noise. We won't have any rooters here tomorrow, so during the game remember it's just a lot of noise and you're not to pay any attention to it. Twenty-five hundred students are back home banking on you to represent the school. You have a big responsibility, and I don't want you to forget it for one second. Come on now — a good night's rest Tomorrow we must win!"

CHAPTER

8

THE FIRST BIG GAME

The day of the game the sun came out bright and warm. There was a tang in the air that was enough to make anyone up at the hour of seven o'clock snap to it. After breakfast, Elmer and Rip took a short stroll around the grounds and they were so impressed by the day, the surroundings, and the occasion that they seemed to walk on air. After their stroll they went back to the hotel, and packed their luggage, and at nine-thirty they pulled out in the big bus for New York City.

The only incident of note on the trip was when they were arrested in one of the suburbs of New York City for speeding. The police officer, however, relented when he found it was the Dulac football team and allowed them to proceed with the warning that they had better stay within the speed limits, as the next "cop" might not be so lenient.

They arrived at their downtown hotel at eleven o'clock, and found the lobby a bedlam. Every Dulac alumnus within a radius of hundreds of miles was there, and as there were a lot of them who had neglected to get tickets for the game until this last minute, the place was loud with exclamations and talk about the gross inefficiency back at old Dulac. It was the old time kicking spirit in full play again, the spirit that makes a man roast his Alma Mater himself, — and want to murder any outsider who does the same. But things soon quieted down, for the student manager of ticket sales had foreseen and made allowance for just such things as this, taking care of the alumni out of a separate allotment which he had stowed away for this sort of an emergency.

The team went down and ate their consomme and toast quickly, and were then all ordered up to their rooms with instructions to lie down until twelve-thirty. At twelve-thirty they were to be prepared to meet in the lobby and get into the busses for the Polo Grounds.

For the first time in his life Elmer felt his knees knocking. A shiver ran through him every once in a while as he lay up in the bed, the portentous first big game occupying all his thoughts. As he thought of the responsibility that would be his at the start of the game, a cold sweat came out on his forehead; he shook all over. It seemed like ages before the phone bell finally rang, and the student manager said, "twelve-thirty! Everybody down in the lobby."

The boys arrived at the Polo Grounds one half hour later, and found five hundred gate crashers, including some small boys there, waiting for their arrival, and hoping to sneak in with the team. It was an exciting scene, but the Polo Grounds manager was adamant, and nobody got in except a few small boys who carried the personal belongings of some of the players into the lockers. The trunks were hastily unpacked and the players dressed themselves immediately.

"There are to be no extra pads on today," the coach announced; "only regulation thigh guards taped on to the thigh, shoulder pads and head gears, nothing else."

At one-thirty sharp the coach sent all his men out on the field to limber up, with instructions to the kickers to limber up their legs and the quarterback to catch the punts and throw them back. The game was scheduled for two o'clock sharp, and at one-thirty there were very few people in the great amphitheater. After ten minutes' work loosening up, the squad all went back to the dressing room, and sat down with their legs stretched out. The coach waited a minute or two; then he announced the opening lineup.

"I want you backfield men to go in there and hammer and tong just as hard as you can for one quarter, and then the regular backfield will go in. Try twenty-one and thirty-three as often as you can, but always kick on the third down. Regarding the center, I want him to make sure of his passes on offense, and on defense I want him to keep moving around, keeping in mind the tactical situation, so that the offensive quarterback can with no degree of certainty know where to find you.

"I want the guards and tackles to charge savagely, offensively and defensively. On offense get under them and lift them; on defense expect every play to come right through your position. I want the ends on offense to get contact with the tackles and stay with them. On defense stay on the outside, and turn everything in.

"Defensive fullback, keep moving; and against running plays hit them so hard that the man carrying the ball won't want to come back again. Learn to run and look at the same time, and don't let them fool you. Defensive halfbacks are responsible for passes, and their key is to watch the offensive end. You quarterbacks have your instructions — do your own analyzing and meet any situation that might arise clearly and decisively.

"Don't forget," the coach went on, passing from specific instructions to general advice, "don't forget that this afternoon, when you are out there fighting, nothing else counts but grit. This is a fighting game and victory always comes to the fighting team. In all its glorious history Dulac has never had a team that has faltered. I think I know you men well, and I feel confident that you are all going to fight as no other Dulac team has ever fought. Two thousand students back at home are waiting for the returns of this game, and while they hope for victory they all have a feeling somehow that we are about to be beaten.

"Let's go out there this afternoon and surprise them. Let's show them that this Dulac team here can hold its head up with any other and will have absolutely nothing to be ashamed of. Let's go out there and play for the breaks. Let the officials do the officiating while we do the playing. But above all we must fight, fight, fight! And if we should happen to get behind, no one must be discouraged. At every turn we must come back with fight, fight, and ever more fight!"

"Let's go!" said the captain, and they were off.

They ran out on the field with a snap and ginger that was thrilling to see. There was elasticity in every stride, tenseness in every jaw, a glint in every eye. A great roar of fifty-five thousand throats greeted them as they trotted out onto the field.

For one little instant, Elmer felt his heart stop still. His whole being was tense with elation. It seemed but a few seconds before the captain came back with the word, "We've won the toss, and kick off to South Square."

Shaking like a leaf, Elmer placed the ball straight up and down and dropped five yards back preparatory to making his running kick on the kickoff. The noise was confusing; it dinned in his ears; he vibrated in every nerve as he thought of the responsibility of kicking off that ball. He heard the referee's "Are you ready?" and then the loud whistle.

Running up decisively, keeping his eye, his mind, his whole sensible body on that ball, Elmer met it squarely and surely, and it flew well over the goal line, for a touchback.

As he lined up on defense, an instant after the kickoff, he was surprised to find all his nervousness gone. With the kick, the tenseness had disappeared with a snap. Now he felt cool and collected. The vast throng of people was just a blur; he paid no attention to it.

South Square was unable to gain any ground on two plays and on the third down the South Square fullback punted sixty yards down the field, and Elmer, focusing his eye on the ball right into his arms, tucked it away and started forward. Two steps, and he felt himself hit just above the knees; the next instant he was flat on the ground. An instant later they were lined up in regular formation, and Elmer barked out the numbers "42, 71, 64, 15, hip." The team shifted and on the next hip, Credon, the left halfback, went inside of tackle on the twenty-one play. A yard was the best he could get. The plunge play by the fullback, number thirty-three, was the next move; it also yielded only a scant yard. Now the South Square line had fire in its eye and it was evident that the yards gained by Dulac this day through that line would be few and far between.

On his own thirty-five yard line Elmer dropped back into the kick formation, and sent a high spiral sailing fifty yards up the field. It was a high punt and the Dulac ends nailed the South Square quarterback right in his tracks. However, South Square was on its own thirty yard line, having gained ten yards in the exchange of kicks. Again the eastern boys started their attack; again they found the Dulac team fighting mad. After two attempts, they once more punted on the third down. This time, however, the kick was short and high, and as he came up fast, Elmer, seeing that the South Square ends were right on top of him, signaled for a fair catch. He held on to the ball on his own forty-five yard line.

As he lined up this time, Elmer saw the South Square halfbacks creeping up closer and closer. Evidently they were totally unprepared for a forward pass. Strict zone play absolutely prohibited passing on the first down; hence their defensive maneuver. Yet, thought Elmer, this might be a good time to throw a forward pass. However, he had his instructions, and again ran ahead with plays twenty-one and thirty-three. Failing to gain, he dropped back and kicked a high spiral slightly to one side; the ball rolled over the goal line for a touchback.

Again the ball was brought out to the twenty yard line, and Elmer noticed instantly that he had made up the ten yards which he had lost on the previous exchange of kicks. To his surprise, South Square punted this time on first down; standing on his own ten yard line the South Square punter lifted a clean kick of seventy yards. Elmer, standing on Dulac's twenty yard line, caught it. The South Square right end took a long dive at him, but missed him, as Elmer side-stepped and starting up the side lines was not stopped until he reached midfield.

By this time, Elmer was a mass of living brain and nerve, every inch of him coordinated, every fiber of him set for the one and only end of it all, a touchdown. Oh, for a touchdown!

Lining up once more, he noticed the South Square halfbacks on defense again drawn up very close. But he was ready for anything. Nothing could stop him now. And then came the inevitable Shorty Dunne and the three regulars trotting out to replace the shock backfield. With a pang in his heart, although with marked relaxation from the responsibility of the strain, Elmer went to the side lines. But that pang was short lived. Another minute, and Elmer was once more electrified with the joy of the game, for, before he had pulled on his sweat shirt he heard Shorty Dunne, with first

down ten, in midfield, call for a forward pass. An instant later the
Dulac left end caught a long forward pass well behind the South
Square halfbacks, who were totally unprepared for it, and with a
few more strides the Dulac end crossed the goal line for the first
touchdown.

Coach Brown came over and sat down by Elmer.

"We had seen all we wanted," he explained, "and besides I was
afraid the South Square coach would chase those halfbacks back
there a little later, so I sent Shorty in there to take advantage of the
weakness right away."

Elmer smiled, his whole heart in his eyes as he looked into the
coach's face. "Touchdown," is all he could say. He was a happy boy.
"Touchdown" — and he had helped make it.

The regular Dulac backfield later also found the South Square
line defense impenetrable, and the rest of the half became a punting duel with no advantage on either side. Encouraged with hope
at their success so far the Dulac boys went back into the dressing
room, between halves, filled with enthusiasm. Coach Brown had
them lie down at full length for seven or eight minutes and there
wasn't a word spoken. After about eight minutes the coach quietly
began telling them that they had to go back in and fight harder
during the second half, as the South Square team was sure to come
back with a punch.

"Let's take no chances this second half; we are seven points to
the good, so let's play it safe. Let South Square take all the chances
and we will be out there playing for the breaks. Shorty, when you
have the ball, kill time as much as you can, and you won't have to
kick until the fourth down, as Jonesey kicks so fast they will never
block one of them in the world. So let's go out there now and stop
them dead, kill time, kick, and play for the breaks. And let us play it
absolutely safe."

They went back out to the field.

South Square came back with a punch, making three first downs
in a row, but in midfield they were stopped dead. Then began a
kicking duel which lasted until the fourth quarter. Getting the ball
in the last quarter, in their own territory, South Square began throw-

ing passes promiscuously, in all directions; but the alert Dulac players continued knocking them down. Finally, in desperation, the
South Square quarterback threw a forward pass straight out toward the side lines, a very dangerous thing to do, and Shorty Dunne,
coming up fast picked it cleanly out of the air and ran sixty yards
for a touchdown. That was a sight that made Elmer, sitting on the
side lines, swell with delight.

Dulac kicked goal again, making the score fourteen to nothing.
South Square came back valiantly and through superhuman effort
developed sufficient power to march to the twenty yard line. Here,
time being almost up, South Square tried a place kick, but failed;
and at that moment the gun went off, ending the game.

Elmer was never so enthused in his life and he ran out on the
field and hugged Rip in his joy. The Dulac alumni surrounded
the team and congratulated them, and it was fifteen minutes before Elmer was able to make his way through the crowd to the
dressing room. There were no injuries, and everyone was happy
and delirious with joy. The team ate at the hotel that night, as
guests of the local alumni, and that evening went to a theater party
where they had another surprise, with Will Rogers, the inimitable
comedian, giving the Dulac team a couple of send-offs in his famous monologue. Elmer had heard somewhere that the ordinary
man had but three or four supreme moments in a lifetime, and he
felt certain this Polo Grounds experience must surely be one of
his. Tired but happy the boys boarded the train at midnight, and
soon the steady churning of the car wheels put him and his teammates to sleep, safe, sound, and victorious, homeward bound after the first big game.

CHAPTER
9

IT'S ALL IN THE GAME

Monday afternoon the team began active practice for the Kingston game and the startled Varsity were surprised to find the Freshmen already well entrenched in their knowledge of the Kingston attack. They mobilized this attack savagely, and that evening after practice whatever tendency towards ego the Varsity had was rudely dispelled. The Freshmen, by their bellicose attack, had severely impressed on them the caliber and worth of the Kingston team.

"It certainly looks to me as if we wouldn't have much time for gloating over our last victory," said Rip.

"The way the Freshmen went through us tonight shows we've been a little stuck on ourselves; we'll have to get over it," Elmer answered. "I suppose it will be our turn to scrimmage tomorrow. And say, did you notice Durley out there this afternoon, just as nice as pie?"

"Oh, why spoil the evening by mentioning his name!" exclaimed the big curly headed tackle, as he proceeded to disrobe for bed. "Durley's not the Dulac type of man. He doesn't fit in here at all."

Elmer finished the letter which he was writing home, and then joined Rip in slumber. The next day the morning mail brought both him and Rip a happy surprise, an invitation to each of them from the president of the Fellowship Club. This club was purely an eating club, the members all taking their meals together in a certain building, where they had their own chef. It was not a fraternity, and while the club was a little exclusive nothing existed which tended toward snobbery. The several dining clubs of the university included in their personnels the leaders in the various activities, and these clubs in no way impaired the atmosphere of democracy around old Dulac.

"Whoopee for honors!" Elmer shouted as they read their invitations.

"I should say we are honored!" Rip exclaimed, as he slapped Elmer on the back.

"You write the club president," said Elmer, "will you, Rip? — and accept for both of us, with many and sincere thanks, and put it nice now, you old dub!"

The food of the commons had been good, and they would probably eat there again, but this invitation from the Fellowship Club was too flattering a thing to think of passing up. It showed that these two boys were lifting their heads before the multitude. They went to their first club lunch that noon and found half a dozen other chaps also taking their first meal there. The members of the Fellowship Club were warmly cordial in their welcome, and Elmer felt a sense of comfort and relaxation as he sat down in the clubroom after lunch and "fanned" with the other fellows on the big things of interest to the student body. Several faculty men ate at the Fellowship Club, and one of them was Professor Noon. Elmer had an idea that probably Professor Noon was responsible, more than anyone else, for his admittance.

As the second team lined up for scrimmage that afternoon, Coach Brown again placed Durley in the backfield with Credon.

"Gosh, wouldn't that get your goat!" said Elmer to Credon.

"It certainly does," replied Credon. "That fellow gives me a big pain in the neck."

"Well," advised Elmer, "let's not pay any more attention to him. We will take care of our jobs, and if he doesn't take care of his, why should we worry?"

The Freshmen ripped up the second string team in great shape that afternoon, and in fifteen minutes had scored two touchdowns. Electrified to activity, the second team came back and marched down the field to the five yard line in an irresistible fury. The next play Elmer called was a plunge by the fullback, in which Elmer's duty was merely to protect to the side. In the midst of the play he suddenly felt a body hit him right on the knee from the side. A twinge of pain shot through his leg up past his hip, and he collapsed to the ground. But quickly, as he went down, he turned his head and out of the corner of his eye he saw Durley rolling away and finally rise to his feet. It was Durley, then, who had done it — one of his own college mates!

Elmer tried to get to his feet. His right leg wouldn't move. The first man to notice him was a Freshman back.

"Higgins is hurt!" he yelled.

An instant later Elmer heard Coach Brown's voice as he ran up to him. "What's the matter, Higgins? What happened?"

As they helped Elmer to his feet it was evident to him that no one had seen the incident. His first impulse was to blurt out the truth, but he checked himself just in time.

"I don't know," he said. "Somebody clipped me from the side."

"Walk around," advised Coach Brown. "Maybe it will work out."

Elmer tried to take one step, but it was no go. He would have collapsed but for the two men holding him up. Old Dad Moore, the trainer, and two Freshmen helped Elmer over to the hospital, where he was comfortably put to bed awaiting the arrival of the doctor.

The doctor, arriving shortly, made a brief examination, then twisted the knee so that Elmer howled in pain.

"The internal cartilage is badly torn, but I just put it back in place. Some of the ligaments are torn, too, I am afraid. You won't be able to play any more football this year."

"Couldn't I possibly get in by the time the last game is played against Aksarben?" pleaded Elmer.

"Well, maybe so," the doctor answered soothingly.

"But let's forget about that for the present. You have absolutely got to stay off this knee for at least two weeks — but maybe the knee is not nearly so bad as we think."

Life in the hospital was not at all as hard as Elmer feared. The coach and the members of the team came up every evening, also the chaps from the Fellowship Club. He received good care and fine meals, and spent quite a bit of his time reading his law books.

Both the Fellowship Club and the football squad sent him up flowers, and fruit, and there was also a bouquet from Estelle Wilson. He was surprised that she still remembered him, as he had not seen her since the previous spring. The only thought which bothered Elmer was regarding the folks at home. Coach Brown had talked to the local reporter, and the only story which ran in the paper was to the effect "on the second team Quarterback Higgins had been replaced by Edwards," with no further explanation. This gave Elmer a chance to write home and explain that he had received a slight injury and for them not to worry at all, as he would soon be fit and active again. The home folks evidently took him literally, for Mr. Higgins even wrote to the effect that "now that you've failed to make the team, you ought to quit it entirely, and concentrate on your law work."

Elmer read all the magazine and newspapers which were brought to him, and the sporting news from downstate which was full of the gloating accounts of the great team State was having under Coach Smith. It boomed Hunk Hughes for All-American halfback, and Coach Smith was hailed as the miracle man. With every word that Elmer read about Coach Smith he ground his teeth, and cursed his own bad luck. He received the returns of the Kingston game by radio in his own room, and the seven to nothing victory he hailed with delight. The team to him had personality and soul, and he was with it in mind and spirit if not in body. As the account of the game came over the radio, he played every play with a fervor and intensity that both shocked and delighted the hospital staff.

Two weeks after he was injured he was able to walk out, but the knee was weak and had practically no strength. He attended his classes that day, and that afternoon he put on a suit again and appeared on the field.

"I'll just play around for about a week," Elmer said to Coach Brown, "because this knee of mine feels rather perky, and the doctor says I mustn't do anything with it for another week or so, so as to give it a chance to strengthen."

"You do just as the doctor tells you," said Brown. "And be very careful with it. And, by the way, I want to go over and have a chat with you one of these nights — I have something important I want to talk to you about."

At eight o'clock that very evening there was a knock at the door and Coach Brown strode in, carrying some papers in his hands.

"I want to talk with Higgins here, alone," said the Coach.

"You betcha," responded Rip. "I'll get right out of here and go next door;" and out he went.

The coach sat tapping with his lead pencil on the papers for a moment before he spoke. Finally he said, "Higgins, if I ask you a fair question, will you promise me to answer honestly, and with no attempt to cover anything up?"

"Certainly!" replied Elmer. Cover anything up? He had no idea what the coach was driving at.

"Was the man who clipped you from the side, the time you were hurt, Durley, your own halfback?"

Somewhat frightened, Elmer hesitated; then he stammered. "Uh, uh, I think it was."

"Can you say for certain?" Coach Brown's eyes were piercing right into Elmer's soul. "This is a very important matter and I must know."

"Yes, I am certain," Elmer finally replied. "But I hope you don't think that I'm a tattle-tale."

"This is no time for false heroics," snapped the coach, "for here I have a letter from the Aksarben coach, in which he states that he received anonymously a copy of our plays and signals. He enclosed them with the remark that I ought to know about it, as there is evidently a traitor in camp."

"No one could have sent these plays out except someone on the squad, as my own coaches are absolutely loyal. We are lucky that the Aksarben coach is a gentleman or this would have ruined our chances for the game. As it is, I intend to change the system of signals, but not until I have made sure of the culprit.

"I didn't see the play in which you got hurt, but I heard about your fight with Durley. I also left Durley at home at the time of the Kingston trip and reports came to me of some very low criticism which Durley has made of me personally. As I said, I didn't see the play in which you were hurt, but I did notice how pleased Durley was later in the day, after you were hurt. I believe he is our man and in fact, after what you say, I am sure of it. However, I do not want you to breathe a word of this to anyone."

Brown went a few minutes later, and he was scarcely gone before Rip was back in the room.

"What did the coach want to see you about?" he asked Elmer, all curiosity.

"He was just inquiring about my knee," lied Elmer.

"Umph," said Rip, "it's funny he couldn't inquire about your knee in my presence."

"I promised not to say anything," apologized Elmer.

"Huh," said Rip, "I'll find out some way or other, and I have a sneaky feeling in the bones that this has something to do with our cold-blooded friend Durley."

Elmer made no reply, but he knew that his face was giving him away to his chum. The rest of the evening was spent in silence.

Only two unimportant games remaining before the big game with Aksarben, the team was working rather easily now, and no one took things more easily than Elmer. One warm night, however, his knee feeling fairly good, he was racing after a forward pass, as they were informally playing around the field, when he felt something pop in his knee and the next instant he was lying prostrate on the ground. As he tried to get up he found that his right leg was just as useless as ever, and a twinge of pain shot through the knee and the full length of the leg. That night the doctor told him that he would need another week of complete rest, though he could go to his classes on crutches.

"You better scratch football entirely for this year, and it may be that in another year your knee will be o. k."

Elmer's heart sank at that, but he tried to take the situation philosophically.

"There's no use fighting about this sort of thing," he said to Rip. "All I can do is make the best of it."

CHAPTER
10

SOCIAL CHAMPIONS AND OTHERS

The night of his second accident, Elmer hobbled over to see Professor Noon, to explain to him why a substitute would probably do the sweeping in the Science Building for the next week or ten days. The kindly old professor was very sympathetic.

"I believe in athletics for the young man," he said, "but not to extremes. From what you have told me regarding your injury I believe the wise thing for you in the future is to confine yourself to such sports as will not endanger the condition of your knee."

"The doctor," Elmer explained, "said it will be all right by next fall, and I'm going to play it safely and take it easy until then."

"I don't like to dash cold water on your hopes," said Professor Noon, "but if I were you I would prepare myself mentally for the probability that possibly you will never play football again. I say that in all seriousness. You are just a youngster, and you have a fine future in law ahead of you, as your professors tell me that you have a legal mind and a fine presence and forethought when you get up to talk."

"Thanks," Elmer answered modestly; "but I just can't help it. Professor! I'd give anything to make that football team next year. I think it would do me the world of good to satisfy that one ambition. I know it would give me confidence in whatever I tackled seriously afterwards."

The old professor leaned back in his chair, strumming his fingers on the table for a minute or two. "I believe that athletics are all right, up to a certain degree," he said. "One of the primary functions of a college is to help a young man *find* himself. There is no doubt that a lot of fine traits of character are developed by athletics. However, it is not an entity in itself, and if I were you I would merely get interested in some other activities; go out a little more socially, and keep your mind occupied so that you won't miss your contacts on the field. And it may still be that you can play next fall; but it is good philosophy to always be prepared for the worst."

Elmer went back to his room that night so discouraged that only the most intense concentration on his studies saved him from a complete case of the blues. He studied hard that night and the night following. The third night, however, he found his thoughts wandering.

"Gee," he suddenly remarked to Rip, turning to that young man who was busily writing a letter, "this inactivity is getting on my nerves! I've got to be doing something, or I'll explode."

"Stars are supposed to have temperament," replied Rip dryly. He always enjoyed teasing Elmer a little. "But I don't see where you have any right to be developing any such symptoms."

"What a nice friendly roommate you are!" exploded Elmer. "When I talk to you again, I'll let you know." And he went to bed.

The next noon at the Fellowship Club, Rip came over smilingly and slapped him on the back.

"I'll tell you what let's do, Elmer, let's take in the Fellowship Club formal next week."

"But I have no girl friend."

"No, I suppose not," said Rip. "However, there's a shy young lady whom you have been neglecting terribly for the last year or so, who might be persuaded to waste an evening with you, and I am the man who will persuade her, so it's all fixed. Here we go."

The Fellowship Club gave formal dinner dances several times a year, and this was the first one of the present season. At six-thirty on the evening of the dance Rip came driving up in a car. He walked into the room with a flourish.

"We're all ready," he exclaimed. "Let's go."

"What's that thing you have out in front there, and what's it for?" queried Elmer.

"It belongs to a friend of mine, and we're taking the girls to the hop in it," replied the big tackle.

"But I've already ordered a cab," Elmer explained. "And besides, isn't it rather an affront to ask girls to ride in a contraption like that?"

"Cancel the cab," said Rip, "and shut up, and come along. These secondhand cars are all the vogue, and the girls will think it's a jolly lift — in fact the first time I get fifty dollars I'm going to buy one of my own. Furthermore, we can't afford to be paying five dollars a lick for cab bills, as long as we have friends who are good enough to loan us a conveyance."

Elmer looked over the contraption and found a big red lantern hanging on behind, two spare tires tied on the top, a lot of curt phrases painted on the body, and hung on behind a sign, "In every day and every way I am growing weaker and weaker."

"All right," he said, after he had hesitated a moment. "Crank it up!"

They stopped first at the house where Rip's friend lived, and when she came out and saw the car she laughed gaily. "My, right up to date!"

"Nothing's too good for the ladies!" was Rip's jolly retort.

Arriving at the Wilson home, Elmer pressed the button with beating heart, and found Estelle all dressed and waiting.

"My, I haven't seen you in goodness knows how long," she said, as she gave him her hand in greeting.

"Well," stammered Elmer, "you know how it is with us football men."

"Yes, how is it?" queried Estelle.

There was an awkward pause.

"I understand you have been hurt again. I'm sorry."

Elmer stammered his thanks. They approached the car, and he wondered what Estelle would think of it. But she, too, joined heartily in the fun of it all, and the next instant they were whirling along the road toward the downtown district.

The dining room at the hotel was beautifully decorated, as were also the tables, making a handsome setting for the Fellowship dinner. At first Elmer was somewhat ill at ease in the conversation during the dinner; it was Estelle who had to take the initiative.

"What are you going to do with yourself, Mr. Higgins, now that you won't be able to play any more football this fall?" she asked.

"It was quite a blow, and time does hang heavy on my hands."

"He will probably be down to see you real often, now," blurted out Rip. And this last remark threw Elmer completely off his social stride again. He gave Rip a look which spoke, "Help me out!"

Rip, however, seemed to be enjoying himself immensely. After an awkward pause, Rip was at it again, "Wouldn't it be a good idea, girls, if Elmer took both of you to the Aksarben game?"

"It would certainly be a pleasure," quickly spoke up Elmer, though the very mention of the game, following Estelle's inquiries about his injury, set the old train of thought going in his head again. Would he be ever able to play again? Had Professor Noon told him the horrible truth? Estelle's voice broke his revery.

"I am sure it would be delightful," she said, while Rip's friend volunteered that she would "just love to go."

After the dinner there was an intermission of fifteen minutes, while the tables were being cleared away for dancing. Although neither Rip nor Elmer smoked, they both excused themselves and went out into the alcove and joined the men gathered there in groups.

"I could have killed you," said Elmer to Rip. "You know I am no 'lady's man.'"

Rip laughed. "You are all wrong on this blushing bashful stuff," he said. "They like them bold and fearless. Say anything that comes to your mind — they never take you seriously anyhow."

"Well, I'm not made that way," said Elmer. "The more I think of it the less I like this job of taking these girls to the game."

"Shucks, it's just what you need," Rip continued. "Don't take them so seriously. Just go around a few times and your point of view will change entirely."

"That may be all right," said Elmer, "but please, for the rest of the night, no more of this airy persiflage at my expense."

However, Rip's remarks did do some good, for Elmer forgot himself completely during the rest of the evening and had a jolly good time. He became truly unconscious of himself until after the dance and the four of them piled back into the so-called car. Although quite a few of the other chaps had cars of a like model and vintage, Elmer could not help but feel that it would have been much more appropriate to have spent some money for taxicabs.

"I have just had a lovely time," said Estelle. "You boys and your crowd are so delightful that one cannot help but enjoy them. Come over and see me some evening when you are not too busy, won't you?"

"Thank you," said Elmer, rather lamely, "I shall." But in his heart he knew he lied. He knew he would never have the courage to go all by himself to see Estelle; and yet, as if against his own wishes, he caught himself wishing that in some way or other his bold friend Rip might sometime arrange a mutual affair which would bring them all together again.

Several days later, at noon, Rip brought the information that Durley, for reasons unknown, had left the university. Elmer never got any first-hand information about this. Naturally he was glad that certain things that he knew of were nipped in the bud; yet in his heart he was sorry and disillusioned to find that there were boys in the world who wouldn't play the game fairly. On several occasions he was tempted to ask the coach about it, but after deliberation he decided that whatever information the coach wanted him to have he would volunteer himself. Coach Brown never mentioned the matter again; and in his heart of hearts Elmer admired him deeply for that. It was a life lesson in reticence that Elmer never forgot.

The same night that brought news of Durley's leaving, several boys in the same dormitory came over to tell Elmer and Rip that they had run across quite by accident, a bunch of very unsophisticated freshmen whom they had decided to initiate into the imaginary Order of the Black Cat. Elmer wasn't able to go along on account of some cramming he had to do for a law class, but Rip went and came back with the report that supplied a lot of fun at the expense of the freshmen.

"The poor saps paid in fifteen dollars apiece, three of them, which makes a total of forty-five dollars. This, I presume, we will use for a special feed. Each one of the candidates had to go over to the Gym blindfolded and stripped save for a towel, and carrying a dead black cat. We gave them the violet ray machine on the chest. We also burnt some hairs under their nose, while we pressed a piece of ice against the skin. You would have laughed your head off to see the way they jumped! They thought surely they were being branded with a red hot iron. Then we made them climb through a row of barrels, put end to end, coming through either side. They had a terrible time passing each other blindfolded."

"Aren't you kind of ashamed of yourselves, to take fifteen dollars away from each of those poor kids?"

"Not at all," said Rip. "All of them have money — that's one reason we picked them. They can charge it to education. Believe me, when they wise up they'll appreciate that they received a liberal education very cheaply. These greenies have to be wised up some way or other. We may as well be the ones to do it."

"Well, the next time you have something of that sort, I hope I can get in on it," said Elmer.

"Well, we have another live one on for next week — a real one. A few of the fellows are nursing him along. They've styled him the marble champion."

"The marble champion?"

"Yes, the marble champion. What do you think of that? In quizzing one of these freshmen one day, one of the boys accidentally found a young gent whose only claim to fame in his grammar school and high school days was the fact that he was much feared whenever the boys played marbles for keeps! Think of it, Elmer! The marble champion! Of course, all the fellows got right in on the idea, patted him on the back, and told him he was just the fellow they were looking for. The last marble champion had been graduated, and it looked as though the school would be weak in this form of sport this year. The poor chap fell for it hook, line and sinker, and Wednesday afternoon he is going to play against Jipper Gite, for the championship of the school. Oh, boy!" And Rip exploded, and danced a jig.

"Well, I certainly won't miss that," said Elmer. Jipper Gite was the school comedian, and Elmer could see the possibilities of such a contest.

The following Wednesday at one o'clock they met over behind the chemistry building. There were a thousand students there, and the Varsity cheer leader gave nine rahs for Hericks, the coming marble champion. When the referee introduced Jipper Gite, who was to contest against Hericks, everybody cat-called and hooted him, and Hericks's bosom swelled. He felt he had the whole university back of him. Rip was the master of ceremonies, and called the two men to the center of the ring.

"I demand that we use the Egyptian break," said Jipper Gite solemnly.

"All right," said Rip, and turning around and addressing an assistant he said, "Fix the pool balls up in a pyramid."

The two men lagged for a line to determine the one who would get first shot. Jipper Gite was the winner. Jipper crouched down at the edge of the circle, with his pool ball, and hitting the top ball of the pyramid knocked it completely out of the circle. As he did so a thousand voices shouted "Foul!"

"I never fouled," said Jipper, burlesquing a very offended attitude.

"You fudged," said Rip, and awarded the next shot to Hericks.

Hericks leaned down on the edge of the circle, and picking on the nearest pool ball knocked it out of the circle, a very simple thing to do. He then proceeded to knock out two more, while the crowd cheered vociferously.

"Speech, speech, speech!" called the crowd.

"Since I have won the championship of the school," said Hericks throwing out his chest, "I will now go into training for the big match with the champ of Aksarben. Dulac need have no fear, as I have never lost a marble game in my life . . ."

Another loud cheer broke out at this, but it suddenly stopped for just at the moment up strode the president of the university into the group. The students backed away, so that the president came right up to the place where Rip, Jipper Gite, Hericks and Elmer were standing together.

"I had heard that this sort of nonsense was going to go on, but I wouldn't have believed it unless I saw it with my own eyes." Turning to Hericks, he said, "Young man, don't you know that these fellows here are making a big fool out of you?"

"Oh, they told me about you," retorted Hericks, blandly, with a smile, "and they said you'd be jealous because you were the marble champion when you were in school."

The crowd nearly burst with suppressed laughter.

"Where are you from?" asked the president.

"What Cheer, Indiana," responded Hericks proudly.

"Mr. Ruggles, Mr. Higgins, and Mr. Gite," said the president, as he turned away, "I will see you up in my office in five minutes."

Five minutes later the three culprits were escorted into the president's sanctum sanctorum. The president tried to look severe, but a little "squib" of a smile crept around the corners of his mouth.

"Tell me all about this, Mr. Ruggles — you seemed to be the leading spirit out there."

Rip, very frankly, told the whole case, and explained that they had no harm in mind, just merely a little rough way of enlightening and humiliating some of the freshmen who were too chesty anyhow.

"This must stop at once," said the president. "There is no doubt in my mind but what this young freshman, Hericks, needs a lot of enlightening, but he will have to get it in other ways. I have no doubt that he will be a very much more enlightened young fellow by tomorrow. Boys will be boys, but you were carrying this thing much too far today. It's ridiculous, and it's wasting time. You three boys have splendid records, and I will overlook it this time. But remember, no more of it."

As they passed out and on across the campus grounds all three of them heaved a big sigh of relief, and voted then and there that Prexy was a regular fellow.

"I thought sure it was goodbye Dulac for me," said Gite.

"I felt safe as soon as I saw him smile," said Rip, "and I think he relented when I told him the whole truth. However, this physical examination that we were going to stage tomorrow night is off. I'll take the stethoscope back to the doctor tonight, and we'll return their dollars to those freshies."

"I think you're wise," said Elmer. "Anyone of those fool freshmen might have had you arrested for impersonating a physician, you know."

"Well, I may be wrong," was Rip's final word, "but I do think all these freshmen were getting some good education at a cut rate but I guess Prexy doesn't get our point of view."

CHAPTER
11

FROM THE GRANDSTAND

The night before the Aksarben game all of the hotels in town were overcrowded, and the congestion became greater every hour as the crowds rolled in from all directions. Coach Brown had taken his entire squad out to the Country Club to keep them away from the noise and excitement of the town and school, so Elmer was left alone. Having completed his studying by about nine o'clock, he strolled down town, but found things very quiet except in the hotel lobbies, where groups of alumni and fans stood around discussing the morrow's game.

One look around was enough to satisfy Elmer's curiosity. On the long walk back to the college, he passed Estelle's house, and did his best to get up enough courage to go and ring the doorbell. However, his nerve failed him at the last instant, and he continued on his way out to the college. The various buildings looked like vast ships at sea in the thick gloom as he came up the long avenue. There were very few lights lit; the morrow was a holiday; almost every student was away for the evening. There was something lonely about the place.

Elmer went to his room and lying back in bed reviewed the events of the past fall. He kept wondering why it was that he didn't seem to get any of the breaks in luck. Here was a game tomorrow, where it was reasonably certain that Dulac would beat Aksarben, a game in which, he felt sure, Coach Brown would send out the shock team to play the first quarter. If he had not been injured it would have meant that he would be out there on the field doing that which he

enjoyed above anything else in the world. But no; he was here with
an injured knee; he would have to watch the game from the stands.
It was hard! He felt suddenly as if he had not even had his chance
yet. His work as quarterback up to the time of his injury, while
above the ordinary, had not caused a ripple, and the recurrence of
his injury was not even of enough importance to be noticed. Sick at
heart, he tossed about in his bed, and it was long past midnight
before he finally fell asleep.

The next morning found a thick heavy frost on the ground, and
a snappy tang in the air. The sun broke through the clouds about
nine o'clock and every vestige of frost soon disappeared; it was evident that conditions for the game would be ideal. About
eleven-thirty the Varsity squad arrived on a bus from the Country
Club. Elmer met the bus; he couldn't stay away. He took in every
word, even to hearing Coach Brown give instructions for the entire
team to eat a very light lunch and be back at the Gym in an hour.

"The team is in great shape," said Rip, as he walked toward the
Fellowship Club with Elmer, "but Coach Brown seems to think we
are a little over-confident.

He had a deuce of a time keeping the alumni and the relatives
away from the players last night."

"Yes, I know," said Elmer, "the coach is a great stickler for keeping everybody away from the team until after the game, no matter
who it is. How about Credon? Will he get in the game today?"

"I don't know, for sure," replied Rip, "but I think he will start
with the shock bunch."

"I understand that there are no tickets to be had, and that there
are rumors of scalping."

"Well, here are your three," said Rip, as he pulled them out of his
pocket, "but I surely had a tough time getting them. There must
have been a thousand people out to the Country Club last night, all
trying to get tickets from Coach Brown, as though he had anything
to do with the ticket sale!"

"Thanks, Rip. These are a great load off my mind," said Elmer, as
he carefully deposited the tickets in his vest pocket. "I'll be running
along now," and as he gripped Rip by the hand, "don't forget," he

said, "the walloping Aksarben gave us last year."

"I won't," said Rip, "but too many of the fellows seem to think we are going to have a cinch, to suit me."

Elmer went back to the room, shaved and dressed himself, and rolling up the two army blankets which he and Rip used on their beds, he slipped them under his arm and strolled toward town.

There was one ideal custom at Dulac. Owing to the nearness of the university field, and the lack of adequate parking facilities, everybody from town walked out. Elmer called first for Rip's friend, Ruth, and then, picking up Estelle at her home, they joined the vast army which was slowly making its way out towards Ludington Field. Arriving at the field, Elmer passed by without effort all the venders that were trying to sell the various novelties, though he did finally buy each one of the girls a large chrysanthemum, and, of course, a program. Then they were shown up to their seats.

The seats which Rip had procured for them were in the very top row, on about the forty yard line.

"Don't you think this is rather high up, and a little too far away to see the game well?" Ruth asked.

"I procured these seats up here," Elmer explained, a little uncomfortably, "because these are supposed to afford the best view. The football scouts always sit in the top row, because everything lies out in front of them like a panorama."

"I think these seats are lovely," said Estelle, and the remark pleased Elmer not a little, although it was still apparent that Ruth was not satisfied.

Slowly and gradually the vast stands became filled with the throng in holiday clothes and holiday spirit. Into the east stand marched one thousand Aksarben rooters led by a band in brilliant red uniforms. They had just arrived on a special train. After the Aksarben band had marched up and down the field the Dulac band came in and they had their strut up and down the field playing their stirring march, which had such a swing and a stimulus to it that it gripped everyone who heard it. Elmer felt a thrill of pride in the band, and the old march, as the drum major waved his baton up and down the field.

At a quarter of two the Aksarben cheer leaders suddenly appeared in their bright red sweaters, and an instant later nine rahs for Dulac volleyed across the field. The Dulac¢ cheer leaders returned the salute in an instant, and in another minute both cheering sections were giving their best efforts at one and the same time. There was a lull for a few moments and then suddenly pandemonium broke loose in the Aksarben stands as the three big teams in red came snorting on the field. They ran up and down the field with a speed and dash that spelled determination and boded ill for Dulac. Three minutes later, the Dulac team appeared and Elmer and the girls yelled themselves hoarse, as they saw the old boys in blue tripping up and down the gridiron. The four officials in white flannel trousers and jerseys of various descriptions appeared next, calling both captains to the middle of the field.

"What are they doing now?" Ruth asked.

"Why, the referee is tossing up the coin, and whichever captain wins the toss gets his choice."

"Get's his choice of what?"

"The choice of kicking off or defending the goal. But with this brisk wind I imagine whichever captain wins will elect to take the wind."

It was soon evident that the Dulac captain had won the toss and had taken the wind, the kickoff thus going to the Aksarben captain. The air was filled with such a din and noise it was almost impossible to hear one another's conversation. Close behind, and to one side, in the press stand, could be heard the clicking of the telegraph instruments. The sport writers were sending out to the world the story of the game. In a cubby hole at the very end of the press stand, Elmer could see the announcer from a downtown newspaper, broadcasting the game by radio.

Dulac was all lined up to receive the kick-off — there was a shrill whistle as the referee put the instrument to his lips, and an instant later the Aksarben fullback met the ball squarely and it soared onward right into the arms of Jones, the Dulac fullback. The Dulac team dropped back, formed a wedge for Jones, and behind this flying phalanx Jones was not stopped until he reached his thirty yard line. On the first down Dulac dropped back into punt formation, and Jones sent the ball soaring fifty yards down the field. The Aksarben quarterback was tackled dead in his tracks.

"Why did they kick right away?" asked Ruth.

"That's to utilize the wind to the best advantage," Elmer explained. "Now it's up to Aksarben to see what they can do with their backs up against their own goal line. They can only kick it back, and it won't go nearly as far against the wind."

Aksarben tried two line plays, and gaining but a total of three yards, dropped back on third down, and punted to midfield. Edwards fumbled the ball for an instant, but recovered it, though there was no return. On the first play Credon went off tackle for six yards, and the ball was brought back, and the referee walked back five yards for Aksarben.

"What's that for?" asked Ruth.

"That's a five yard penalty for being offside. There is an imaginary line drawn through each end of the ball, clear across the field. One line is the line of scrimmage for the team which has the ball, and the other line is the line of scrimmage for the team on the defense. Neither team could cross its line of scrimmage until the ball is passed by the center, or there is a penalty of five yards. The team which has the ball dare not be in motion when the ball is passed back by the center. On that last shift play, Dulac was off too fast, and that's the reason for the penalty."

In the meanwhile Dulac had tried a forward pass and this was incomplete. As they lined up, the score board showed second down, fifteen yards to go. Another forward pass went astray; this time as they lined up the score board showed third down, fifteen. The maneuver of trying two forward passes in succession rather puzzled Elmer, and he couldn't for the life of him grasp the reason for such strategy on the part of Edwards. On the next play Jones dropped back in punt formation, and placed a beautiful punt to one side which rolled out of bounds on the five yard line. This feat was greeted with loud cheers from the Dulac cheering section.

"What was so exciting about that, that made them all yell?" Ruth asked.

"Well," said Elmer, "the way it is now, it is Aksarben's ball on their own five yard line. If the ball had rolled across the goal line before it went out of bounds it would have been a touchback. In that case it would have been Aksarben's ball on the twenty yard line so by kicking the ball out on the five yard line, they saved fifteen yards."

"Just as clear as mud," said Ruth.

"Don't say that, Ruth," Estelle put in. "You know it's just as clear as can be."

But Ruth only pouted.

Standing five yards behind his own goal line the Aksarben kicker, on the first play, now hoisted the ball fifty yards up the field, right into the arms of the waiting Edwards. The ball seemed to nestle in his arms and then an instant later it lay squirming on the ground. Like a flash a red-jerseyed man was around it.

"Shucks, we fumbled, and Aksarben recovered — that's a bad break!" Elmer exclaimed.

"What is a break?" Once more Ruth's battery of questions was turned on.

"Well, that's rather hard to define," Elmer answered, "but a blocked kick or a fumbled punt or any kind of a fumble is supposed to represent a break for the team that recovers the ball."

In two plays Aksarben had smashed for a first down, right straight through the Dulac scrub line. On the next play they fumbled, however, and the Dulac center recovered, making it Dulac's ball on her own forty-five yard line.

"Well, that evens it up — that's a break for us," said Elmer.

On the first play Credon for Dulac skirted the end for twenty yards, but the completion of the play found the official standing where the ball had started from, and again the ball was brought back. This time the referee measured off fifteen yards.

"What was that for?" said Ruth.

"That was for holding," gloomily responded Elmer. "The team that has the ball is not allowed to use its hands or arms in any way, and the penalty for doing this is fifteen yards."

"But the Aksarben boys were using their hands — I could see that very plainly," said Ruth.

"Yes, that's true," said Elmer, "but the rules say that the team on defense may use their hands to ward off interferers, while they are attempting to get to the man carrying the ball. It is only the team which has the ball which is not allowed to use its hands or arms."

"Does that mean that the team on defense can slug?" asked Estelle, in wide-eyed wonder.

"No, if the team on defense uses its hands illegitimately, such as striking with the heel of the hand in the face, or slugging, they'll get penalized fifteen yards, and the man may be put out of the game."

Meantime Dulac had again tried two long forward passes, both of which were incomplete, and on the third down Jonesy kicked a long punt down the field, which the Aksarben quarterback caught on his own twenty yard line, sidestepped the Dulac end, and returned the ball ten yards before he was smothered under a swarm of blue jerseys. Starting on their own twenty yard line Aksarben now reeled off three first downs in succession. In one of these plays the officials stepped forth and the referee walked for five more yards for Aksarben.

"What was that for?" asked Ruth.

"Oh, let's keep quiet — I think we're annoying Elmer, and he isn't enjoying the game a bit," said Estelle.

"Oh, that's all right," said Elmer. "I am at your pleasure. Dulac was offside that time, Ruth."

"Thank you," said Ruth, but not without a look at Estelle, whose remark apparently had hit home; for from then on until the Aksarben team reached the twenty yard line, Ruth asked no more questions.

At this point eleven new blue-jerseyed men dashed onto the field, and Ruth joined in with the rest of the vast throng in exhorting Dulac to hold.

"We'll see a different game now," said Elmer, "the regulars are in."

Three plays — Aksarben shot two inside of tackle and one outside of tackle, and not an inch did they gain in the three downs.

"They'll have to make ten yards on the next play or it will be our ball," said Elmer.

He could see the Dulac backfield move back further so as to be in a more advantageous position to protect against a forward pass. The Aksarben quarterback was clearly flustered, and up in the air.

"Well, we have stopped them this time," said Elmer. "Just watch that team go when they get the ball."

At that instant the ball was snapped back by the Aksarben center, and the Aksarben halfback dropped back, throwing a forward pass to their left end, who had run straight down the field to the goal line. Elmer's nerves gave a jump; just then he saw Shorty Dunne leap clean into the air, and bat the ball.

"Good for Shorty!" thought Elmer; and then his heart sank as he saw that Shorty had batted the ball right into the hands of an Aksarben halfback who was coming down the field several yards behind the end. The halfback hung onto the ball and crossed the goal line, while Elmer felt a lonely and empty sensation all the way to the pit of his stomach. The Aksarben team lined up on the five yard line, and executing a perfect place kick added the extra point, making the score seven to nothing in their favor.

"Just a bad break," said Elmer, "just a bad break."

"I know, but it's seven to nothing favor Aksarben."

Elmer said nothing in reply, but he felt that his patience was being sorely tried.

As they lined up for the kick-off, it was apparent the Dulac captain had elected to receive. This time the man kicking off for Aksarben kicked it away over the goal line, making it a touchback, and the ball was brought back to the twenty yard line. As they lined up on the twenty yard line, waiting for the referee's whistle, it was evident that the entire Dulac team was over anxious to get-going — they fairly shook with suppressed excitement.

On the first play, Dulac made seven yards; on the next play ten yards; and as Elmer watched them march down the field he grasped the reason for the use of the long forward passes by the first quarterback, Edwards. On every play the man carrying the ball faked a forward pass and the line plunges and end runs following gained big yardage. The Aksarben second and third line defense lay away back looking for the forward passes which didn't come. Down the field, past midfield, swung the Dulac team, off-tackle, through line, first left, then right, right down to the five yard line.

Then a pistol shot was heard. It was the end of the quarter.

CHAPTER

12

DEFEAT

The teams exchanged goals, and this meant that Dulac would now have the wind against her. Dulac was placed in the same relative position on the other five yard line, and the minute intermission being up the referee blew his whistle. Three different plays Shorty Dunne chose, and the Dulac backs hurled themselves into the line three different times, but one yard on each play was the best they could get; it was now fourth down on the two yard line. The next play, which found Elmer with his heart in his mouth, was a trick pass play.

An instant later a Dulac halfback went sprinting across the goal line, all by himself, and Shorty Dunne threw the ball right into his waiting arms — and he dropped it! There was a groan from the stands that could have been heard for blocks.

"I never saw such a day for bad breaks," said Elmer. "Gosh, I never did see such bad luck!"

"Why didn't he catch it?" asked Ruth.

"He tried to, but missed it," said Estelle, seeing Elmer's rising color.

"Well," said Elmer, "you can't discourage that bunch of men out there — they'll come back yet."

With the wind with them, however, Aksarben chose to play a kicking game the next quarter, and Shorty Dunne, trying to duplicate his first march, found that much of the enthusiasm of his offense had been spent. Nothing unusual happening the rest of the quarter, the half ended, with the score still seven to nothing in favor of Aksarben. In spite of his encouraging words to the girls, spoken as much to encourage himself as them, Elmer felt half desperate.

Between halves one thousand Aksarben rooters in the stands snake-danced all over the gridiron to the intense chagrin of the thousands of Dulac supporters, who sat back stolidly hoping for the best in the next half. A group of Dulac students came out to put on a burlesque game between halves, but with the score seven to nothing against them, their heart wasn't in it and the thing was a dismal failure.

As it was the Aksarben captain's choice the second half, they chose the wind, and when Elmer saw that Dulac had elected to receive, he turned to the girls with determined face.

"The boys are going to take the ball and march straight for a touchdown," he said. "Their ire is up and they won't be stopped, you wait and see!"

Shorty Dunne caught the kick-off on the goal line, and brought it back thirty yards behind perfect interference. The first downs they made by slicing off tackle and line smashing — and then as the Aksarben second and third line defense crept up close, Shorty threw three or four passes, which carried the ball to the fifteen yard line. The Dulac stands were in an uproar.

It looked easy for Dulac now! Aksarben seemed unable to stop them. On the first play on the fifteen yard line, the Dulac fullback went plunging into the line; but an instant later a huge red-jerseyed individual emerged with the ball and went sprinting down the field with no one near to stop him. He crossed the goal line without anyone having come within ten yards of him. There was a stillness throughout all the stands, so still, one might even hear the heart-beats. Even the Aksarben stands could hardly grasp the situation. And it wasn't until they had place kicked for the other extra point that, with a loud howl, they gave vent to their exultation over what had happened.

"What happened?" asked Ruth.

"Well," said Elmer, "one of our backs thought he was carrying a loaf of bread home to mother, and that big Aksarben tackle just

merely took it away from him and ran for a touchdown. Gosh, it
makes you sick when you think of all the time Coach Brown has
spent in teaching this fellow how to carry the ball, and then to have
him go out there and practically give the game away like this!"

"I don't believe Coach Brown can teach anything to anybody,"
said some fellow in front of Elmer.

"What a fine loyal rooter you are," said Elmer. "I bet you've placed
about five dollars on the game and because you're going to lose it
you'll blame Coach Brown for it."

"Why, we should beat Aksarben by four touchdowns," said the
big burly fellow as he turned around and looked Elmer in the eye.

"You can't beat them with breaks of this kind," Elmer retorted,
"and I don't see how you can blame a coach for the things that
caused these two touchdowns."

That silenced the burly critic, and Elmer leaned back; but then
he suddenly realized how embarrassing this must have been to the
girls.

"I'm awfully sorry I paid any attention to that fellow," he
apologized in a low voice.

"I don't blame you at all," said Estelle. "It's just as my father says;
there's no one half so bright or half so brilliant as what he calls 'the
second guessers.'"

"What is a second guesser?" suddenly cried out the irrepressible
and ever-questioning Ruth.

Elmer didn't reply, though the critical gentleman in front again
turned around and gave the three of them a belligerent look.

With the score fourteen to nothing it was evident that the spirits
of the entire crowd, almost all of whom were Dulac supporters,
were very much depressed. On the next play or two, after another
kickoff, there was practically no sound at all, and as the two teams
exchanged kicks it looked as though it was all over but the shout-
ing. At that instant the Dulac cheer leaders, three of them, got out
in front of the stands.

One of them, with the megaphone to his mouth, yelled sharply,
"Dulac, in all its history has never quit — are we going to quit today?" And a resounding "No!" went reverberating across the grid-

iron, as each heart and lusty throat responded to the inspiration of that challenging cry.

That thunderous "No!" must have been heard by the team on the field; for as the fourth quarter started the Dulac boys began their third march down the field to the goal line. Three and five yards to the play they averaged as they slashed, whirled and drove their way up the field. Once a forward pass, good for twenty yards; then back to the running game! Now up to the fifteen yard line again; but here once more they were stopped for short gains three times in a row.

"They'll forward pass on this play," said Elmer desperately, "another trick forward pass!"

And sure enough, as the play developed it found Shorty Dunne ending up far back to one side with the ball in his possession. Suddenly he tossed it to the fullback, who was hiding out by himself in one corner of the field. The silence in the grandstands was breathless.

This time the ball was not dropped. This time the fullback walked across the goal line for Dulac's first score. Shorty Dunne kicked goal and the score was fourteen to seven.

"There's nothing to it. I think we're going to get two more!" Elmer cried in exultation.

Aksarben chose to kick-off and they kicked far over the goal line for a touchback. As the teams were lining up for the first play, the two girls and Elmer heard a lady down somewhere in the front ask her escort, "For goodness' sake, whose ball is it now?"

"Why, it's Dulac's ball," said the man gruffly.

"Oh, goody," said the excited lady, "I just knew they would get it before the game was over!"

Involuntarily Elmer turned and looked at Ruth.

"Now don't tell me I am as dumb as that!" Ruth protested with her eyes flashing.

"As dumb as what?" said Elmer, innocently.

"You heard all right! But never mind, I won't bother you any more."

"Why, yes, please," said Elmer, "any time anything comes up that you want to ask about, please do so, Ruth."

With the same irrepressible rush which had marked their last march, Shorty Dunne took the dashing Dulac team straight up the field for first down after first down, until finally the ball rested on the one yard line, with fourth down goal to make. And as Elmer watched Shorty Dunne he could read his very thoughts.

He thought of a line buck, and saw that huge Aksarben line now massed tight in front of Dulac. The ends were in tight. Aksarben had two backs playing up close, right behind the ends and a little bit on the inside, ready to reinforce whether on line plunges or end runs. Two men only lay back for the forward passes, as they had but a very short territory to cover — the end zone in which forward passes could be caught being only ten yards in depth.

"I'd throw a pass, but Shorty, of course, can tell out there by sensing and feeling the situation a lot better than we can here," Elmer remarked.

True enough, a forward pass it was, the same play that they had scored on previously; and again the Dulac fullback slipped over in a corner all by himself.

But just as Shorty Dunne poised to throw the ball he slipped and fell, and before he could recover, two red-jerseyed men had smothered him.

Elmer groaned. "Ye gods, I don't believe the Fates want us to win this game!"

In trying to maneuver for a better position to kick, Aksarben first fumbled and then on the next play, was thrown for a three yard loss. The next play found the kicker standing eight yards behind the goal line.

"Time out," cried the Aksarben quarterback, and yelling to the field judge, asked how much time was left.

"Three minutes," came the answer. And then, as the Aksarben quarterback lined up to kick, he saw that Dulac had, besides their seven men on the line, the fullback who was up alongside the left tackle. It was evident that they were going to make a desperate attempt to block the kick — a blocked kick would tie the score.

He went back and whispered something to the fullback and then lined up again and began calling out his numbers. As the ball was passed back to the fullback, several blue jerseys swarmed through, but the Aksarben fullback merely touched the ball to the ground and squatted on it. The referee's whistle blew, and an instant later the ball was carried out to the thirty yard line.

The score on the board now read, Aksarben fourteen, Dulac nine.

"Can you beat that!" said Elmer. "Well, I guess it's all over now. They played it safe, and it looks as though they are going to win."

"What was that" asked Estelle, "that counted two points?"

"That was a safety," said Elmer, "the ball being declared dead in Aksarben's possession behind their own goal line — it would have been a touchback if the force came from a Dulac player. However, since the force which carried the ball across the goal line was from one of their own side, it is a safety. The center passed the ball across the goal line. He furnished the force."

"I don't understand what you mean," said Ruth, "but I think it's a darn shame for Rip and the boys out there to have played so well, and then to be beaten."

"I think it's darn poor sportsmanship," said the big red-neck up in front, turning around to Elmer. "That sort of thing should be stopped."

"It's perfectly all right according to the rules," said Elmer, "and as long as the rules are that way, I don't blame them for taking advantage of them."

"Well, Shorty Dunne should have hit the line for that fourth down anyhow," said the other.

"That's all right for the Sunday morning field general," Elmer replied, "but Shorty Dunne had to make his decision out there right on the spot and quickly, and it wasn't his fault that he slipped and fell."

This last remark apparently did not mollify the man, at least it silenced him.

The Aksarben team now rushed the ball with great vigor for one first down; then they ran their plays off so slowly that they still had the ball on the third down when the gun went off announcing the end of the game.

Elmer and the girls made their way slowly out through the exits, and over towards the gym, where they were to meet Rip. Scarcely any words were exchanged between them. A little later Rip joined them; and it was evident that he had been crying. They looked at him in frank astonishment. No one had ever seen Rip like that before.

"I had hoped that we could go out to dinner together," he managed to say, "but the way I feel, I think it would be best for me to go home and sleep it off."

"I think that's a perfectly good suggestion for tonight," said Estelle, "but for tomorrow I'd say, let's all four have dinner at my home, and I won't take 'No' from any of you. By that time Rip will have gotten over the game of today, and we can have a jolly good time together."

"I may appear to be over it tomorrow night, but I will never really get over today's game," said Rip. "We all played our heads off, but things just wouldn't connect. I guess you understand."

Elmer at least understood — and Rip knew it.

CHAPTER
13
EIGHTEEN MONTHS ELAPSE

The first part of December passed rapidly, and Elmer and Rip settled into their work rather briskly, and with little to break the routine. Elmer made an effort to qualify as a debater, but was not quite able to make it. The few days preceding the holidays were busy ones. All the professors were holding special quizzes so as to make sure none of the boys would take any more time off than that allotted by the faculty. The evening before they left for home, Rip and Elmer, along with Estelle, had dinner at Ruth's house. The dinner was beautifully done, and Estelle was more lovely than ever, and yet Elmer's interest was dulled for some reason, and the boys went home early. The next day Elmer boarded the local train which took him back home to Springfield.

The return of the conquering hero is always an occasion for pomp, brass bands and revelry. The return of Elmer to Springfield produced not even a ripple of conversation anywhere, except in the Higgins home.

"You are certainly looking fine, Elmer," said Mrs. Higgins, as she embraced her boy.

"Yes," said Mr. Higgins, "and I just had a letter from Professor Noon, who says your law work is very encouraging."

Elmer appreciated to the utmost the fine home he had, and during his two weeks Christmas visit he did everything he could to show his parents little attentions and courtesies. There was a special "Father and Son" meeting at the Kiwanis Club, and this he attended with his Dad, not failing to notice the pride Mr. Higgins took when, on introducing Elmer, he announced, "My son, Elmer Higgins, home for the holidays, from Dulac." Abner Hughes came up a minute later, "My son, Hunk Hughes, home for the holidays, from State." The sincere round of applause which followed showed that the citizens of Springfield were not blind to the fact that the great playing of Hunk Hughes at the state university was good publicity for their town. Coach Smith of State was also introduced, and gave a short talk in which he explained why he was a great coach.

"The people like bunk," thought Elmer, "but I don't believe they can stand it as a steady diet."

After the meeting was adjourned that noon, Smith came over and shook hands with Elmer.

"I see you didn't have very good luck in making the team at Dulac."

"I was doing pretty well," said Elmer, "but I had my knee hurt, so I didn't get into the last games."

"That's too bad," was Coach Smith's rejoinder, made with a rather insinuating tone, as he walked away with some friends.

To Elmer's consternation, he overheard Smith remark to these friends, "As a coach, I surely hear a lot of funny ones. This young Higgins boy just said he didn't make the team at Dulac on account of a bad knee. Hah! he hasn't got any bad knee; he's suffering from a goiter in his neck."

Elmer felt so furious that he hardly could restrain himself from following Smith and having it out with him face to face. However, he held his temper, and went over and joined Hunk. They went out together.

Elmer and Hunk were inseparable friends, and spent most of their free time together during the two weeks' vacation, and of course they discussed Smith.

"I know he's your coach," said Elmer to Hunk, one day, "but by George, I can't stand him! I know he has made several insulting remarks around town about me, but he'll find out that I'm no quitter. The only reason I ever want to make the football team at Dulac, is to show him."

"Oh, he isn't a bad fellow," said Hunk, "but you have to understand him."

"I'm afraid you don't understand him," Elmer answered. "He's pretty foxy. He takes all the credit for your great playing himself, and gives you none. He is the greatest 'self-interest' fellow I ever knew in my life."

"Now, I wouldn't say that," said Hunk. "Personally, I think he's all right, but since you and I are good friends, let's not discuss him any more."

Elmer admired Hunk for his loyalty, so it ended there. The name of Coach Smith didn't come up again during the holidays.

Dropping in at the corner drugstore one evening, after a movie, Hunk and Elmer each had a soda. There was quite a crowd of town boys in the place. Included in this group was a chap who was known as the town josher. Walking up to their table, he remarked, so that all the crowd in the place could hear, "Well, you'll be going back to school again soon, Hunk, and I want you to know that the whole town is proud of you, and we are all watching you. We are all sorry that you hurt your knee, too, Higgins. I didn't see you limping, and so didn't know anything about your sore knee until Coach Smith told me about it."

Elmer heard a giggle run through the crowd, and so paid no attention to the innuendo in the remark. To his relief he saw that Hunk was totally unaware of what was referred to. However, to Elmer it was apparent that Coach Smith must have been doing quite a bit of joking around town in his own insinuating way about the injury, and he determined then and there that if he ever did anything in his life he would get into the game that Dulac would play with State the following fall. He was determined to avenge himself personally, and to humiliate the swaggering Smith. In fact, Elmer became so worked up over the situation, emotionally, that he found himself waking up at night, worrying about the game that fall. He confided to his mother all his hopes and fears, ambitions and humiliations; she was the only one who seemed to understand him.

"Your father isn't very keen about your playing, Elmer, but I understand how it is, and I certainly hope that you take good care of your knee, and that you can achieve everything that you have your heart set on."

"Well, the way it is now, mother, Coach Smith has me painted here in our home town in entirely false colors, and I think that I owe it to you and Dad, as much as to myself, to show that we can hold our heads up with anybody."

It was with that set purpose that he returned to Dulac at the close of the Christmas holidays.

But alas for determination! Before many months had passed, Elmer was doomed again to disappointment. Running for a university street car one day his knee popped out, and he was laid up for several days. Still he was not discouraged. With the routine work of the spring over, he obtained a job for the summer as a life guard at a bathing beach, feeling that this was not only the kind of work which would give him time during the summer for reflection, but, more than this, it was exactly the thing for his lame knee, for old Dad Moore had told him that the heat of the hot sun on the beach might heal up his injury.

Then, once more, came a set-back. Returning to school after his uneventful but restful, and very beneficial summer, he had gone out for practice only one day when, out popped the bothersome cartilage again! This time he was laid up for three more days; and at the end of those days came the final verdict.

"Young man," the doctor told him, "your football days are over, and I shall inform Coach Brown of this fact."

Something seemed to crack in Elmer's heart at these words. For a moment he was stunned. But on the instant he turned stoic. And stoic he remained, all through the following year, when at every game he was forced to stand on the sidelines; forced to sit in the grandstand, while the great State team was held to a tie by the light, fighting Dulac players. He read in the papers of the various alibis of Coach Smith, explaining why the top-heavy favorite team of State had not won. He read in the papers how the Dulac team had once more beaten South Square. He devoured the news of the surprising victory of a weak Aksarben team over Dulac. And all this, naturally, had its effect on him. At times he became extremely moody; he went mostly by himself. He saw very little of Estelle. Rip, of course, did all he could to cheer him up; but, though Elmer outwardly appeared to be quite settled and adjusted to things, within him were smoldering fires, which would not out.

One day in May, Professor Noon sent for him to come to his study room.

"How have you been feeling, Elmer?" asked the kindly old professor, after he had asked Elmer to take a seat.

"Just fine, professor; how have you been?"

"Same as usual," said the old gentleman, settling back in his chair, apparently deep in thought.

There was a long silence; then finally he drawled out, "I have been watching you for some months, Elmer. Apparently there is something wrong; and I have come to certain conclusions."

Elmer wondered what he was in for.

"Your law work has been falling off a little," Professor Noon went on, "not much, it is true, but falling off. Your enthusiasm seems to be gone — you seem moody, — gloomy. You don't mix with the other boys; in fact, you have become a little cynical, I'm afraid. Now, I believe that your class work here is bringing you some knowledge of law; at least you are learning to concentrate. I do believe that you have a good mind and that you have patience, will power, ability to analyze. And I believe, too, that you have pretty fair control of yourself.

"However, I have come to the conclusion that you are so set on making this football team that I am afraid if you don't make it, you are liable to make a fizzle of life. I have never been particularly keen for athletics, but I do appreciate that under Coach Brown it has qualities for character development. He insists that you men play the game fairly and squarely. He doesn't coach from the side lines, thereby robbing the boys of the opportunity to think for themselves. He insists that every man who represents Dulac shall be clean physically and morally, and must bear well the responsibility which rests on his shoulders.

"I have never heard of any Dulac athlete reflecting discredit on the school. I have come to believe that the young men who play football do develop initiative, resourcefulness, ability to analyze, and to react quickly and accurately to this analysis; and I believe, too, that football teaches boys their limitations and their possibilities. They develop respect for an honored opponent. They develop a sense of fair play which in my opinion is one of the hardest things to inculcate into any young man. "Last, and very important, I do believe that the football man develops the *will* to win. I used to believe that this development of the *will* to win was a bad thing. However, we on the faculty are trying to develop young men for life. Life is competition. We are sending out lawyers, and these lawyers cannot be successful unless they win cases. We are sending out doctors from our medical schools and they cannot be successful unless they win — winning in their case means saving lives. We are sending out men to the business world, and they cannot be successful unless they win. They cannot be successful if they go into the bankruptcy court; and this is generally what happens when men lack the *will* to win.

"So I have come to look upon athletics, properly controlled and supervised, as being a thing that will help to develop character. I think we are coming to the day when we are not going to penalize the successful man who wins in anything so long as he wins fairly. We are going to penalize the cheater, and I know that Coach Brown in Dulac University doesn't tolerate a cheater for a moment."

Professor Noon paused a second. Elmer was taking in every word — for every word was a confirmation of his most earnest belief.

"The function of the college," the professor continued, "the undergraduate part of the school at least, is to help a young man find himself. Now, apparently, we have failed in your case, as you seem entirely lost and out of touch with yourself. And now for the real point of my having you over here.

"I have a friend, Doctor George, in Chicago, who has performed some very remarkable operations on knees. Would you be willing to go up there as soon as school is out in June, and submit yourself to an operation by him?"

"Would I?" said Elmer; he sat bolt upright as he answered. "Gosh, I'd take a chance on anything! It seems too good to be true. I can hardly believe it."

He shook the old professor's hand eagerly and gratefully as he went that night.

"How can I ever thank you for this interest you have taken in me, and for this great favor? I assure you, Professor Noon, I never shall forget it."

The second week in June, school being over, Elmer journeyed to Chicago, where he met the great surgeon, and had the operation performed. His pal, Rip Ruggles, had been elected captain of the team for the following year, and this fact only added to his determination to get back into football at any cost.

CHAPTER
14

SECRET PRACTICE

On the fourteenth day of September, that next fall, there was a long line of young men standing around one end of the gymnasium. It was about half past two in the afternoon, and the hot September sun was just beginning to lower itself into the horizon. Many of the young men in line were in their shirt sleeves on account of the heat. The green of the leaves was just beginning to turn to a browner shade. There was that in the air which warned that summer was over and that the crisp autumn days would soon be here.

In the inner office of the gymnasium, somewhat removed from the room where four student managers were giving out football suits, checking lockers, and making notations, sat Coach Brown. Before him on the desk lay several pieces of paper on which were the names of all the candidates who were to be out the next day. There was a knock on the door.

"Who is it?" inquired the coach.

"Rip Ruggles."

"Come in." Rip entered. "What's on your mind this afternoon, Rip? Did you get your suit and locker all right?"

"Yes, Coach, I'm all fixed up and raring to go tomorrow, but these student managers won't give Elmer Higgins a suit."

"No, I gave them orders to give suits only to those men on the list. We're a little shy on equipment, and I'm giving out only to those who I think have a chance to make the team. Higgins has that chronic knee of his, and there's no use of his wasting any time over here."

"Well, I have some good news for you, Coach. Higgins had his knee operated on in Chicago in June and it's just as good as ever now."

"How do you know?" Coach Brown sat forward.

"Well, in the first place I saw it, and tried it. And yesterday afternoon we played three sets of tennis and that sudden stopping and fast starting didn't bother it at all."

The coach remained deep in thought for several minutes; finally he said: "Well, now, that might be a solution. We lost Shorty Dunne a year ago, and last June Edwards graduated. I tell you what you do, Rip; — you go out and get Higgins and send him in to me here now, right away — and also get hold of Ward who handles our publicity."

Ten minutes later in together came the two young men. Elmer, brown as a nut, had an appearance of rugged suppleness that bespoke good condition. Ward was a typical student correspondent, nervous, high-strung, and bubbling over with enthusiasm. Coach Brown greeted them cordially; then suddenly, without a sign of warning, he hit Elmer a resounding whack on his right knee. It almost felled him.

"Don't be surprised, Ward; I was just wanting to assure myself about Higgins' knee. I understand you had a little operation last June, Higgins?"

"Yes, I did, Coach, and I was laid up only three weeks, and since then I've been down at the beach as a life guard. My knee is just as strong as it ever was, and I have never felt better in my life."

No emotion showed on the inscrutable face of the coach; he turned now to the newspaper correspondent.

"The reason I sent for you, Ward, is to tell you to keep everything concerning Higgins absolutely under your hat. In our first two practice games against Alba and the Normal team, Higgins will not appear. There will be secret practice every night, beginning with the first practice tomorrow. This will continue up until the Aksarben game. Aksarben has beaten us two years in a row, and Higgins here will be my trump card. So don't forget — regardless of what you see in the daily scrimmages, or practices, there must be no mention of the name Higgins.

"Higgins, here is a note for Wherrett, the student manager; he'll give you full equipment. I'll see more of you later."

An hour later Rip and Elmer were winding their way up and down the ravines along the shore of the historic creek.

"Gee, it surely seems good to get back to the old place I hate to think of ever leaving it," said Rip.

"Yes, we do a lot of crabbing while we're here, but I appreciate more what Professor Noon said now."

"What was that?"

"He said that the four years a fellow spends at college are the best years of his life. I wouldn't have said so last spring," continued Elmer, "but the way I feel now, it seems I have a new hold on life."

"You could have knocked me over with a pin when you told me about your knee," said Rip. "Why the deuce didn't you write and tell me about it?"

"I didn't tell anybody except my mother. I was optimistic, but I wanted to be sure before I said anything."

"Shucks, you could have told me."

"Well, I wanted to surprise you."

"You certainly did surprise me, all right. I guess Coach Brown is mighty tickled, too, though he doesn't say so. He was in a pretty tight hole, as his other candidates for quarterback don't amount to very much. This last year's Freshman quarterback, Berlin, is being touted quite a bit in the papers, but all I ever saw him do is drop kick. He certainly does that with a vengeance, but that let's him out."

They got to a high point on the bank of the creek and stood for a few minutes overlooking the beautiful country below them.

"Let's cut straight across the fields for the four-mile road," said Rip, "and we can gather some grapes at the school farm on our way back."

"That's a go," said Elmer, and a minute later they began trudging their way leisurely across the fields towards the university farm.

"What do you think will be the hard game this fall?" said Rip, after they had walked for some distance.

"Well, as far as I am concerned, the one game I am living for all fall is the game with State on Thanksgiving Day."

Rip, who knew all the details regarding Elmer and Coach Smith, laughed. "I guess you'd like it if Coach Smith would come out and put on a suit and play himself, wouldn't you?"

"I don't care if we lose every other game on the schedule. If we could beat Coach Smith forty to nothing it would be the greatest day of my life, and as far as I am concerned I'd consider all my efforts at football well worthwhile."

"I thought Hunk Hughes and you were pretty good friends."

"We are good friends — next to you he is the best pal I have. But that has nothing to do with this game of football."

"State, I understand," Rip commented, "has the finest material it has had in years. They have three other backs just as good as Hunk, and that's the reason I know the State game is going to be a battle."

"Smith doesn't know much football," was Elmer's answer, "and all he thinks about anyway is Smith, Smith, Smith. I think he is a detriment to the game, and I think it is men like him who cause some of our faculty men to lift their eyebrows whenever you mention the word football."

"Well, I'm with you with every ounce of energy and pep I can work up and I know you'll have nine other teammates who will be feeling just the same, and you know it, old boy."

"Yes, but you forget, Rip — I haven't made the team yet," said Elmer; "though if anybody makes that position regular at quarterback," he added, "it will be over my dead body."

They filled their pockets with grapes at the farm, eating a bunch or two as they continued their stroll, but saving most of them to be eaten in the room just before bedtime.

They arrived back at the Fellowship Club for their evening meal as usual, and found there the cheerful, serious crowd which had always given the Fellowship Club a distinctive atmosphere. Professor Noon, with several others of the faculty, was present. The conversation at dinner drifted from the League of Nations to the Prohibition Law, and finally to the one inevitable subject of football. Jipper Gite, who was taking some post graduate work, did most of the talking when the last subject came up.

"The team looks all right to me, boys. If Coach Brown can only dig up a quarterback. With Credon and Miller at the halfbacks, and Jones at fullback, we have three of the greatest backs in the country. The line looks very strong and I believe that Ruggles at guard, and Kerr at end, ought to have a good chance for All-American — I trust you will pardon me for getting personal, Rip," said Jipper.

"Oh, I'm good, I admit it — you remember I played a great game for Aksarben last fall," replied Rip, which retort brought smiles to the faces of the club members, for they all knew full well that if there was any man who played football the year before against Aksarben, it was Rip Ruggles.

"The first big test will be against Aksarben," said one of the crowd.

"South Square is not so good this year — graduation raised havoc with their team," remarked another.

"As far as I'm concerned," Elmer put in here, "the team we've got to beat is State. They have the finest material, but that's one game we are going to win."

"I was rather hoping," remarked Professor Noon, "that when we resumed playing State, that our relations would be more pleasant. I understand, Mr. Ruggles, that there was a lot of muckerism in that game last year."

"There was," said Rip, "but they've one boy who is a gentleman, and that's Hunk Hughes, their halfback."

Elmer shot Rip a grateful look of thanks. Shortly afterward the conversation drifted to the new Commerce Library, which had been donated by some wealthy alumnus.

The next day, the opening day of practice, there were some seventy-five men trying out for Varsity. A like number were equipped to try out for the Freshman team. After an hour and a half's work on the simplest fundamentals, the coach let them all get a drink from the pump, and lie under a big tree in the corner of the field for fifteen minutes. At the end of the intermission, Coach Brown came over and began talking.

"Boys, there are certain things which I want you to bear in mind. First of all, I want not a single man to mention to anyone, not even his own roommate, the fact that Higgins is running signals with the Varsity. And secondly, I don't want any man to mention to anyone anything about our plays and signals. Our first big game is with Aksarben, and if anybody asks you what our chances are, in that game, tell them you don't know. And you don't. I am purposely going to make you look bad, because I won't give the quarterbacks any plays to use, but between ourselves we are going to have a good team, — a team that in the Aksarben game is going to surprise everyone.

"I want every man out here to feel that he has a chance to make that team; whether or not he does depends entirely upon himself. We have the men here, we have the spirit, we have everything, in fact, to start a season on. But we have an awful lot of hard work ahead of us, a lot of grief, a lot of monotony. I don't want any man to stay out unless he is absolutely serious, and intends to give the best that's in him.

"If you get tired and worried, don't get discouraged — the test between now and the Aksarben game is going to be severe and only real men will come through. This game of football is very much like warfare, and it's up to you men to see that no information goes out that would be of any help to our opponents. We must spring a surprise in the way of attack, and this can only be done if each one of us keeps his own counsel."

The men fell to practice shortly afterwards with a vim and vigor, and a tearing up of the turf, which showed that the team as a whole was a unit in determination and concentration. Whether or not they had the competitive soul, that fire of nervous energy so necessary to succeed in football, only time would tell.

Ten days after the opening practice, the coach held his opening scrimmage of the season. Jones, Miller, and Credon took turns at some brilliant individual running with the ball, though teamwork and cohesiveness was still lacking.

"It certainly is a God-send that your knee is all right," said Rip that night. "These other quarterbacks are certainly just a lot of number callers. This fellow, Berlin, hasn't got a brain in his head, and all he seems to want to do is to call his own number, to run or pass or kick — and yet the coach didn't say a word to him."

"Coach Brown will never say anything to the quarterbacks in front of the rest of the team. But I expect that on Monday, at the special quarterbacks' meeting, we will be shown all our mistakes in today's scrimmage."

"I understand the students are somewhat up in arms on account of the secret practice," said Credon, who had been up with them since earlier in the evening.

"Aw, shucks," Rip answered, "Coach Brown will explain all that at the first mass meeting, and they will forget all about it as soon as we lick Aksarben. He may hold open practice the day before the Normal game to give the cheer leaders a chance to rehearse their cheers, and everybody will be satisfied.

"I'm afraid the coach is overdoing the gloom stories that are going out, however," continued Rip. "I understand some of the alumni have been writing in, and they seem to be pretty well worked up and worried."

"That's a good way to have them — we'll give them the surprise of their lives on October seventeenth."

The next week was a series of feverish scrimmages, mostly on offensive play, getting the team ready for the Normal game. The reports on the Normal team were meager, but there was nothing to indicate that it had anything more than its usual team. During the week a dozen plays were rehearsed, dummy scrimmage was practiced by the hour, and the first two teams scrimmaged a full hour with the plays on Tuesday, Wednesday, and Thursday. The entire squad heaved a sigh of relief when Coach Brown ordered a little light workout on punting and receiving kicks for Friday afternoon. Jones was punting sixty yards, with good height, and even Elmer was getting the ball out around fifty yards most of the time. Coach Thrown worked quite a bit developing the wedge formation on the kickoff, and also the fake wedge.

That evening Coach Brown called a meeting of the quarterbacks for six-thirty in his office in the gymnasium.

"I don't even want you to put on a suit tomorrow, Higgins. I want you to sit on the bench and draw a chart of the game and make a written report to me by Monday, of what you would have done in the various situations, had you been up against a team as strong as Aksarben.

"Mull and Berlin, I want you to go in there and work just three plays, twenty-eight, the inside tackle play; ninety-two, the wide end run; and fifty-six, the little short forward pass. I want Credon to throw that out to the flat zone to Miller. Credon is not a very good passer, and this kind of a pass will make that more apparent. Neither of you two men can forward pass, and I want the both of you to try to throw a couple of passes to the ends on punt formation, without any signal. I want all the visiting scouts to see the fact that neither of you two quarterbacks can pass.

"Higgins, here, is passing better every day, and by the Aksarben game I want the Aksarben team to feel that our forward pass attack is below the ordinary. Berlin, when you are in there running the team, I want you to try a place kick, whenever you get inside the thirty yard line. I want to build you up all year as a place kicker."

The coach then went on and gave a list of routine instructions, after which he dismissed the boys.

"I wish I could run the team the way you do," said Berlin to Elmer, as they walked back toward the dormitories.

"The same here," said Mull. "There are so many things a quarterback has to think of that I don't know where to start or where to finish."

"You just take the things as Coach Brown hands them to you," Elmer answered, "absorb them and retain them, and keep building up and you'll get along all right. I have had practically a year's experience, which you haven't had, and which Coach Brown seems to consider as being of some importance. However, I don't want you fellows to feel that I have any edge on you. You fellows, so far, are going just as good as I am, and the thing for us to do is to go out there and be good friends, and work together for Coach Brown, and let him pick whoever he thinks is the best man."

Both Mull and Berlin thought this was fine on the part of Higgins, a senior. This marked the beginning of a strong friendship between the three of them. There were no petty jealousies among them at any time during the season.

The next day, Saturday, proved wet and dismal. There was a steady downpour all day, but despite this there was a big crowd out to see the team in its opening game. The three weeks of secret scrimmage had whetted the appetites of all the fans to a fine edge, and there was much speculation in the stands as to who would be playing quarterback. Coach Brown started Berlin with the second team, and after about fifteen minutes of play, consisting almost entirely of kicking, the Normal quarterback fumbled and the ball was recovered by the Dulac left end.

"Now is Berlin's chance to see what he can do," said Elmer, who was sitting in civilian clothes next to Rip. The first play failed to gain, and on the second play, Berlin fumbled, but recovered.

"He certainly looks all up in the air out there," said Rip.

"He'll make this place kick, though," said Elmer, as the Dulac team dropped back on the thirty yard line for a place kick formation. The next instant Berlin stepped forward and meeting the ball squarely sent it sailing between the uprights, making the score three to nothing.

The Normal team chose to kick off, but as the Dulac team was lining up to receive, eleven new blue-jerseyed players arrived on the scene. Elmer sat back on the bench, and to him it looked as though it would be just a matter of form as to whether or not the Varsity would score two touchdowns or four touchdowns the next quarter.

Down the field, ten to twelve yards at a clip, came the Varsity; and then, just as it seemed as though the score was a certainty, Mull forward passed right into the arms of a Normal player.

"That was a boner," said Elmer to himself.

The Normal team lined up and kicked the ball fifty yards up the field on the first play. Again the Varsity started up the field, but this time found the going much harder. Encouraged by their success thus far, the Normal team was playing away over their heads.

It was now Dulac's turn to kick. Held for no gain on the third down, Jones sent a spiral fifty yards back up the gridiron. The Varsity found themselves unable to make any consistent gains at all for the rest of the quarter, and the half ended with the ball in their possession in midfield, Berlin's place kick still constituting the lone score.

Nobody seemed worried between halves, as the Normal team had not shown any offense, and there were no signs that they had anybody with any offensive ability.

"I think we'll play it safe this second half," said Coach Brown to the team. "You go back in there with the same team, Mull, this third quarter, and I want Jones to kick continually on third down. Play it absolutely safe. Whatever you do, Mull, don't throw any more of those short passes this half.

"This Normal team is fighting like the deuce, and will probably come back harder than ever this second half. This certainly is just the kind of practice we want and a lot of you fellows who think you are pretty good better get a different point of view on the game this second half. This Normal team isn't running out of the park just because you fellows go out there with eleven Dulac headgears. There is only one way to make this game safe this second half and that is to go in there and play as though you meant it. Our ends, particularly, are pitiful. You have been lying around on the ground on your stomachs so much that you must feel like a lot of bathing beauties out on the beach being photographed for the rotogravure section.

"The tackles and guards have got absolutely no charge, and all our backs seem to be thinking of is making a long run for a touchdown. Long runs for touchdowns are all right. However, the safest way to insure a touchdown is to keep biting off the four and six yard gains."

At the start of the second half Dulac received and marched the ball right down to the ten yard line, when for some unaccountable reason Mull forward passed again and the ball was grounded in the end zone for a touchback. The Normal team put the ball in play on the twenty yard line, and punted on first down.

"Berlin, you go in there," Coach Brown ordered.

Out onto the field went the sprinting Berlin, to report to the referee. Mull came over to the sidelines, rather crestfallen; but Coach Brown said nothing. Elmer went over and sat down by Mull.

"What made you forward pass again, right down there when your running attack was going so well?"

"Miller suggested it," said Mull.

"Don't pay any attention to any suggestions from anybody," said Elmer. "You're the quarterback; you're responsible for all offensive plays, and you're the one that's going to be criticized now for the mistakes that have been made."

"I know it," said Mull. "It certainly won't happen again."

In the meanwhile down the field the Varsity was again flying, five to eight yards at a clip. Berlin was using himself quite frequently and when they reached the ten yard line, Berlin, on a quarterback sneak play, fumbled the ball. The ball was recovered by the Normal team, and their cool headed punter, on their first play, sent the ball back past midfield, with a clean high soaring punt. The Varsity became discouraged, and there was no more ground gained the rest of the third quarter.

In fact, the game was a succession of punts until well along in the fourth quarter, when, standing on his own twenty-five yard line, Berlin dropped a punt and the wide awake Normal end pounced on it like a flash.

"We certainly aren't looking very good today," said Elmer. "If the Normal team has any kind of a place kicker now, they'll tie the score."

Walking up to Coach Brown, who sat at the other end of the bench, Elmer inquired, "Should I go in and put a suit on? I can get dressed in five minutes."

"No," replied the coach, "we'll stick to our original plans, regardless of what happens. The Normal team has no offense, and I'm not worried about stopping them."

"I know, but how about a place kick?" asked Elmer.

The coach said nothing, but it was plain that he was worried.

Three different plays the Normal team tried, but they were held for no gain in each instance by the Dulac line, which was now charging in with a vengeance. The Normal team took time out, after which they lined up in place kick formation. They were directly in front of the goal posts; the quarterback kneeled down to receive the ball from the center on about the thirty-two yard line, and it was plain that if the Normal team had a good kicker it would be a tie score.

"Block that kick," yelled the Dulac cheering section.

However, as soon as the Normal quarterback started calling his numbers, the Dulac cheering section quieted, due to the tenseness of the situation, and also for the sake of courtesy.

Back from the center shot the ball, and like a flash the quarterback held it on the ground. An instant later the fullback had met the ball squarely, and it was soaring toward the goal post. However, it swerved away and missed by more than a yard.

"His foot described a lateral arc," said Elmer, "or he would have made it."

"A miss is as good as a mile," replied the coach laconically. "If Berlin gets away a good punt the game is over."

Standing on his own ten yard line, the ball having been brought into the twenty yard line from the resulting touchback, Berlin kicked the ball sixty yards and two minutes later the game was over.

CHAPTER
15

"INTERFERENCE"

That evening after supper Rip announced that he had made an engagement for Elmer and himself to go to Ruth's home that evening. Yes, Estelle Wilson would be there, and they would either go to the movies, or they would enjoy themselves at home singing, for with Ruth at the piano, this was one of their favorite pastimes.

The boys arrived at Ruth's shortly after eight o'clock, and found that the girls had already made some fudge and were in a merry mood. Rip suggested going to the movies, but Ruth pleaded that she was too tired, having been out to the game that afternoon. So they stood around the piano and sang for a short while to Ruth's accompaniment.

"I think you were rather selfish," said Ruth to Elmer, later on in the evening, "not to take us out to the games."

"Coach Brown has a special reason for having me on the bench," Elmer answered, blushing, and with evident embarrassment.

"Special reason?"

"But I can't tell you anything about it until after the Aksarben game," he hastened to add, still more embarrassed.

"Are you sure," asked Estelle, smilingly, "that you aren't using that as an excuse not to go with us?"

"I know Elmer is bashful," Rip put in, "but I can assure you that he is on the bench for special reasons, and we are only sorry we cannot say anything about it until after the Aksarben game."

"This sounds terribly intriguing," said Estelle, "but I can t possibly imagine what it can all be about."

"I do wish that Elmer had a good knee, though," said Ruth, "because he certainly could play better than those quarterbacks this afternoon. My Dad said that was the worst game he has seen Dulac play in twelve years. He also said that Aksarben will beat you by four touchdowns, unless there is a decided improvement somewhere along the line."

"There'll be an improvement, all right," said Rip; and then he managed to change the subject. "Let me hear you play that rhapsody again, Ruth, won't you, please? I think it's wonderful."

Shortly afterwards Estelle left for home, Elmer, of course, her escort. Rip went with them a short way, going on to the university at the corner where Elmer and Estelle turned for her home. Bidding good night at the front door, Elmer finally mustered up courage to say, "I really'd like to take you and Ruth to the game next Saturday, if I can arrange it with the coach. Maybe I won't have to be on the bench for this game."

"I'm very sorry," Estelle answered, rather casually, "but I already have an engagement for the game. However, I'd be pleased to accompany you to the Aksarben game, if you like."

Elmer felt himself growing red with embarrassment. 'I'm sorry," he stammered, "but you see I won't be able to take you to the Aksarben game." Of course, he couldn't explain; he felt horribly foolish! "But," he added, "I can arrange with a personal friend of mine to go with you and Ruth."

"Please don't bother," was Estelle's answer, and Elmer felt its coolness. "Good night." He felt dismissed.

Practice the next week consisted of a series of scrimmages in which the Dulac Varsity, led by Elmer at quarterback, concentrated entirely on their offense.

"Our defense," remarked Coach Brown, Thursday afternoon, "can take care of itself. Defense is largely a matter of individual courage, aggressiveness and technique. Offense is the difficult thing to develop, because it is entirely a matter of teamwork. The finesse of timing, judgment, and team coordination are very difficult to attain. I am far from satisfied with what has been shown so far this week. Aksarben will have all her scouts here so we'll have to go out and beat Alba Saturday with the same three plays we used against Normal last Saturday."

The game the following Saturday against Alba was in many respects a repetition of the Normal game. Once more Elmer sat on the sidelines and saw the Varsity, with Mull at quarterback, march for a touchdown in the first five minutes. Against the reserves in the second quarter, however, the Alba team presented an impenetrable defense, and the usual punting duel resulted. Just before the whistle blew for the half, Dulac fumbled and an Alba player, picking up the ball, ran seventy yards for a touchdown. They kicked goal, a thing which the Dulac Varsity had failed to do, and the score at the end of the half stood seven to six in favor of Alba.

In the third quarter Alba rose to real heights and continued to hold Dulac with apparent ease. It was not until the fourth quarter, when, goaded into a frenzy of desperation by apparent defeat the Varsity, now led by Berlin at quarterback, marched sixty yards down the field to the five yard line. They were still using only the three plays which they had used in the Normal game. Here, however, Alba again put up a stone wall defense. On the fourth down Berlin went back into punt formation and standing on the fifteen yard line place kicked for three points. Alba kicked off again, Dulac was starting another march down the field, when the game ended.

Elmer, getting up from the bench, found that he was tired even more tired than he would have been had he played. Dulac had barely won nine to seven; it was a close call. Walking back toward the gymnasium, he came alongside Coach Brown, and here noticed for the first time that the coach looked tired and careworn.

"That was pretty hard on my nerves," said Elmer to the coach. "It's a lot harder to stay on the sidelines than it is to be in the game, by far. Weren't you worried at all?"

"Yes," Coach Brown admitted. "I had just got to the point where I was going to send out a substitute with instructions to have the team open up the full offense, when suddenly they got going without it. I'm glad we didn't have to use our offense. The Aksarben scouts are now completely in doubt as to our style of attack and the system of offense."

"But Aksarben has an easy game also, so we won't know much about their offense, will we?"

"No," Brown replied, "but it won't matter much. Our plan next Saturday will be to get hold of the ball and to keep possession of it all afternoon. Aksarben won't be able to beat us as long as we have the ball and are scoring. Unless I'm mistaken we'll do very little punting next Saturday."

Elmer waited for Rip to get dressed, after which they made their way together toward the Fellowship Club for dinner.

"Well, there's no date tonight for us, old boy," said Rip. "I called up this noon and Ruth said that she and Estelle had other plans."

"What difference does that make?" But Elmer, in his heart, knew that it did make a difference. "We can get in a few rubbers of bridge over at the club," he went on, "and by that time it'll be bed for me."

"Oh, I suppose so," Rip agreed. "But as a pair of ladies' men we are a couple of clowns. Did you see the two sheiks that were with the girls this afternoon?"

"No."

"Well," said Rip, "they're two of the prettiest boys in school. One of them has a nice blond mustache, and the other fellow wears a big raccoon coat."

"Well, what about it? You aren't jealous, are you?" "No, not exactly; but if I'm going to be turned out I'd like to have it done by men, and not by a couple of flossy boys."

"Well, if they're the kind of fellows the girls prefer, I don't see where it concerns us," said Elmer.

"Maybe it shouldn't," replied Rip; and then he continued with some determination, "I'll have an engagement with Ruth for next Saturday night if I have to shave a certain blond mustache, or buy a raccoon coat myself."

As Elmer lay in bed that evening running over various things in his mind, for the first time he felt more and more upset about the day's happenings.

"But what right have I to get sore?" he asked himself. "I have no right to dictate in any way with whom Estelle shall attend the game, or with whom she should associate. We are just good friends, nothing more."

And yet his pride was stirred, and his thoughts, as he lay awake, were not on football.

The next Monday noon the blackboard drill was called off, to the surprise of the entire squad. When they went to look for Rip to find out why it had been called off, they were informed that Rip and Coach Brown had gone to attend some special meeting. Neither one of them appeared on the campus all that afternoon. The workout that afternoon was conducted by one of the assistant coaches, the two leading assisting coaches also being missing. And this on the Monday preceding the Aksarben game! What was up?

Elmer tried to analyze the situation, but all he could do was to speculate and only hazily at that. Instead of the active organized practice, with one single end in mind, the work that afternoon was entirely informal. When it was over, about a quarter to six, Elmer dressed and hurried to the Fellowship Club. Sure enough, there was Rip. At a glance Elmer saw that something had happened. This was a different Rip than the one he knew. The usual carefree attitude of his roommate was gone, the happy-go-lucky air was missing, and so was the irresistible smile. The glint in the eye, the set of the jaw, and the quivering of the mouth showed that from the crucible of some emotional reaction there had emerged a new byproduct, a new compound, which Elmer didn't understand.

"What's the dope, Rip?"

"Sssh, I'll tell you after dinner."

"Why the intrigue and mystery?"

"Now, don't be a sap," said Rip. "Let's keep quiet until after dinner, when we can get into a quiet corner, and then I'll give you all the dope — and believe me, you'll hear something that you will want to digest slowly."

Dinner over, Rip and Elmer found two chairs in a corner of the writing room, and making sure that no one was near, they sat down for their talk.

"Well, what's it all about?" asked Elmer. "I've been trying to dope it out in my own mind, but not having any facts, I'm absolutely at sea."

"Well, it's a long story," Rip began, "but I'll make it as short as possible. This noon there was a meeting of the Advisory Committee on Football, and I, as captain, and Coach Brown, were invited in. Only two of the faculty men were present. The rest of the men present were alumni. I could see as soon as I went in that the spokesman for the alumni was Windy Bill Biggs, — you know, the millionaire fish magnate from the Pacific Coast. You remember he was a great player here in his time, and he's now the chairman of the Alumni Advisory Board."

"What is this Alumni Advisory Committee, anyway?"

"I don't know their exact duties," Rip answered, "but somehow or other they must have a lot of authority, judging from the way the faculty kowtows to them. Windy Bill didn't waste any time, but came right out with the announcement that the alumni were entirely dissatisfied with the coaching, and entirely dissatisfied with the showing of the team the first two games this year. He was empowered, he said, to come down with the rest of the alumni committee, either to make a change in coaches, or to put some assistant coaches in from among the old timers. These assistant coaches were really to run the team, to get it in shape so that they could win the big games of the year."

"And what did Coach Brown say to this?" asked Elmer, his eyes wide with surprise.

"Nothing — he never said a word; just sat there, quiet, and apparently disinterested. But you can bet your life I didn't keep quiet. I asked Windy Bill what he knew about the situation, and he told me to keep quiet and not to be so impertinent, as undergraduates were to be seen and not heard. That made me sore, and I came back at him. I told him that if he followed his own advice they would have to change his nickname. Oh, he was wild — threatened to put me out of the room, and all that sort of stuff; but I reminded him that I was captain of the team, and that we were eleven men who would stick together as a unit.

"We let him talk for a long time and they had all kinds of plans for bringing back some of the old timers. Finally, when they just about had their plans ready, I began talking again, and told them that before they decided on this plan of theirs, that they might have the courtesy to listen to Coach Brown. Coach Brown, I told them, had a plan he had been working on all fall, and since his profession was that of a football coach, maybe he might have a few remarks on the game that would be of interest, even to these experts present.

"Windy Bill gave me a glare at this, but he did have the decency to ask Coach Brown to give his views. It was after four o'clock by that time, and the coach got up and began talking very quietly. He told them first of all that he didn't know much about the fish business, and so he wasn't in a very good position to give advice along that line to Windy Bill. I tell you I was surprised and happy at that, because I thought the coach was down, the way he'd been sitting there all afternoon. You can bet your life all of them started pricking up their ears after that first remark of his.

"The coach then went on to explain that he had been coaching at Dulac ten years and during that time had lost just five games, a record which was surpassed by only one or two in the coaching profession. He went on and told the crowd that many times in the past few years Dulac had won games when they were not supposed to have a chance. He told them that nobody, except himself and the team, knew how it was done. He explained the two defeats in succession by Aksarben, by giving full credit to Aksarben, asking whether or not he was to blame because men fumbled, or didn't hold on to forward passes. Then he explained about your knee, Elmer, and all about his strategy in preparing for this game for next Saturday against Aksarben. He said he appreciated the interest taken by the alumni, but just the same he wound up by saying that he thought it would have been better if the alumni committee had asked him about his plans first, and not waited until this late hour. In fact, he said, he realized that the only reason he was called upon to explain was because Captain Ruggles had suggested it.

"There was a lot of pow-wowing after that, but you can bet they listened to me when I told them that the team was with Coach Brown to a man, and they were just as loyal to their school as they were to their coach. I told them that if they didn't let Coach Brown alone for this Aksarben game I wouldn't be responsible for anything that might happen.

"So they finally adjourned, and postponed action until after the Aksarben game. That's the story. Elmer, what do you think we ought to do?"

"I would do this," said Elmer, "unknown to the coach, or the alumni, or anybody else, I'd call a meeting of the fellows for tomorrow night, and tell them just exactly the facts as they are. I think if we can do this the team will go into that game against Aksarben so fighting mad nothing can stop them."

"All right! It's a good idea. I'll have the dozen fellows meet over in our room tomorrow night. We can squeeze them in some way. I don't think we'd better bring any more fellows than a dozen, or the meeting might become public property."

The practice the next afternoon was as different from the practice of the day before as one could imagine. The coach was energy personified. He was all over the field at the same time. During offensive scrimmage every detail which went wrong was rectified. They spent an hour and a half polishing up the forward pass plays, which were to be used against Aksarben. Elmer was the passer in all these plays, and as he threw the ball right into the arms of the receiver again and again his confidence in himself grew and mounted to a pitch of enthusiasm.

That evening about seven-thirty some twelve football men huddled together in Elmer's room, with Rip as master of ceremonies. Rip explained the facts as he had explained them to Elmer.

"Now, here's the point, boys," he exclaimed. "The alumni have no business butting in at this time of the season. They'll ruin the whole fall if they do, because they don't know what they're talking about. Secondly, we all know that Coach Brown is as good a man as the school can get, and it's up to us to see that the school retains him. Thirdly, all the football we know we have learned from Coach Brown, and we all know we have a great team coming along. It would be absolutely unfair for someone else to come in here and take credit for this work.

"However, the big thing we want to bear in mind is this — we all know Coach Brown's plans and we believe in them. We're going to go out and win every game this fall. So, let's all shake hands on beating Aksarben decisively next Saturday, so that Coach Brown and the team can go right on with the campaign this season, un-hampered by a lot of busy-bodies. If they want to change coaches between seasons that may be all right, but it's altogether wrong to be butting in at this time of the year."

The boys rallied to Rip's talk wholeheartedly, and swore to fight to the last ditch the coming Saturday afternoon.

"Remember," said Rip, just before they left, "this is absolutely secret, and no one must ever hear of it. I just thought we could represent old Dulac with more intensity and fervor next Saturday, knowing the facts as they are."

The next day at noon Rip told Elmer that he had arranged with Ruth and Estelle to attend the autumn dance to be given by one of the university clubs the evening after the Aksarben game. Elmer concealed his interest as much as he could.

"I don't know who these two fellows are that are trotting after them," said Rip, "but I call them Dan Dormitory and Joe College. Ruth was rather peeved over the phone when I called them these names, but believe me they give me a big laugh. They're taking the girls to the game Saturday. I had quite a time arranging for the dance engagement. However, I dropped a couple of hints that aroused their curiosity, about the game Saturday, to such an extent that they decided to go to the dance with us and not with the two anecdotes. Believe me, I know these women! Just rouse their curi-osity, and you have them where you want them."

Elmer couldn't help but laugh at Rip's "women wisdom," and his candor in talking about it.

When the practice Thursday evening was over, the men were called in together by the coach for a short talk, after which they were all dismissed. Every man was in good shape physically and even Coach Brown was surprised at the spirit which the team was showing.

"I've been coaching for many a year," he remarked to Rip, "but I've never seen a team so ready for a game as this one."

"You'll get the surprise of your life during the game, too," said Rip enthusiastically. "This is one game I wouldn't worry about if I were you — it's already in the bag."

The coach smiled. "The time to win the game is Saturday afternoon."

The regular meeting of the quarterbacks was held Thursday night in the coach's office, but by this time the number of quarterbacks had been cut down to three. Mull and Berlin had been showing up much better in practice, but even these two ambitious young gentlemen had to admit that it was a different team entirely with Elmer running it.

But in spite of all these high spirits, it was evident to Elmer, as he sat in the office, that the coach was worried keenly. He tried to cover it up, and Elmer admired him for that; but the telltale evidence was plain in the deep lines of his face and the intensity of his voice.

"Now, in this game Saturday," said the coach beginning his talk to the quarterbacks, "we've got to get the jump early. Let's get Aksarben on the run and keep them there. We don't know much about their style of play this year, but we do know that they have a veteran team. Lord, their right halfback, is a terror on offense. He's the man who has beaten us the last two years.

"We do know, however, that he is absolutely helpless against the forward pass. We will start the first team against them — and Higgins, I want you to forward pass over Lord's head on the first play, and to continue passing over him whenever you think the situation is ripe. Don't forward pass on third down or on second down. In this game, we're going to forward pass on the first down, thus violating all the rules of strategy that are generally accepted in the game. After we have scored twice, and I have every confidence we will, then I believe that our running attack will go, as the Aksarben team will be entirely demoralized and will be running around panicky, trying to stop the forward passes. These, however, from that point on will be withheld. There is only one thing I want you to bear in mind on defense.

"Besides being a great ball carrier, Lord is also a great receiver of forward passes. Why he is so vulnerable against forward passes when he is playing defense is beyond me, but getting back to my main point, Lord is a great receiver of forward passes. He is the man who runs deep. Therefore it is the quarterback on defense because he is the man playing farthest back — who will have to cover him on all forward passes. Don't let him get past you. This would be fatal. We'll continue to play an offensive game of football all through and if any of the men tire out at all, Rip will let me know so that we can keep putting fresh men in there all the time. We must go at full speed every minute of the sixty."

Friday afternoon the team merely played dummy defense against the Freshmen, who used the Aksarben formations as they interpreted them. The team then practiced returning the kick-off a few times, after which they went back to the gymnasium. The workout was extremely light, just enough being done to put on the finishing touches that were needed. All through this Elmer was surprised to find that instead of being nervous he was filled with a deep determination and a confidence in himself which he had never before experienced. In fact the whole team seemed to feel the same way. Rip was the only exception. His duties of captainship were beginning to act a little on his nerves, but his powers of leadership were still at their best.

16

THE COMEBACK

After dinner on the memorable Friday evening before the Aksarben game the entire squad of thirty-five men were loaded into busses and taken out to the Country Club. Elmer found the Country Club a delightful place at this time of the year, not like a club at all, but like a huge country home; for there was no one there but the caretaker. A bright fire was burning in the big open grate, so as soon as the boys had put their luggage away in their rooms they came down to the main hall to sit around and enjoy the comfort and satisfaction which comes from a log fire; all the more so since it was already quite cool out doors in the evening. Spending their time at cards, the victrola, and in good natured talk around the fire, they put in a happy and restful evening. The trainer, Daddy Moore, was a great believer in having boys keep their minds off the game, and he was around in this group and that, busying himself telling stories and in general keeping them in good humor.

Everyone was up for breakfast at seven-thirty. It was an ideal day.

"Our forward passing game ought to go great,'" said Rip at the breakfast table. "Our main forte is speed, but I would hate to think of playing that giant Aksarben team in the mud, — but then, why worry about mud.? — we'll run them ragged today because they haven't anybody fast enough to catch Miller or Credon."

As the boys took a walk around the golf course after breakfast, Dad Moore smiled to himself. It was evident that every man had the color, and the suppleness of muscle, that denotes perfect physical condition. It was also evident to Dad's experienced eye that the team as a unit was absolutely right mentally, in exactly the state of mind men should be in before a game. There was no playfulness in their mood this morning. That was all right the night before; but now they were serious and recollected. There was a grim silence as the groups walked along.

"There will be no lunch today," said the trainer, Dad Moore. "The whole crowd of you are so nervous and keyed up that I am afraid to feed you anything."

So the team waited at the Country Club longer than had been expected. They left in busses so as to reach the university gymnasium about one o'clock. Arrived there, they began dressing immediately. The halfbacks and ends had the thigh guards taped directly on to the thigh. The halfbacks and ends also had their ankles taped. The linemen had their wrists taped. Dad Moore rubbed one of the linemen's legs with wintergreen. This lineman had been suffering from a charley-horse, but had recovered. The wintergreen was added here merely to keep the leg warm, and to prevent it from becoming tight again and hence more susceptible to another charley-horse.

At one-thirty, the team was all dressed and all three centers sat nervously playing, each with a football. There was no one in the dressing room, but the team, Dad Moore, the student managers and the coach. The assistant coaches were all away scouting. Just at this moment, in through the door came a delegation of men, at the head of which was Windy Bill Biggs. Coach Brown greeted them with a smile and shook hands all around.

"I'm glad to see you here today, gentlemen. Boys," and he addressed the team, "these men here are all alumni who have come a long way to see Dulac play Aksarben today."

Windy Bill pulled the coach to one side. "Do you mind if a couple of us talk to the team before the game?"

Elmer overheard this with astonishment, but he was not surprised at Coach Brown's response. "Nobody talks to the team except myself," said the coach. "You men mean well, but you don't understand."

"Why, man," protested Windy Bill, "Lou Harmonica, the greatest jury lawyer in America, is with us, and he could send that team out there in a state of mind where they would fight their weight in wildcats."

"I'm sorry," said the coach firmly, "but I have made it a policy never to allow anyone to talk to the team except myself."

"Well, it's your own funeral, not mine," and Windy Bill turned and made his way out the door followed by the rest of the alumni group.

At a quarter to two the coach called for silence, and then he surprised the team by making the shortest talk on record.

"I want a silence of one minute," he began, "absolute silence, while every man here prepares himself for an hour of the hardest playing he has ever done in his life."

The silence that followed was indeed profound; it lasted not one minute but several; the place was tense with it. Finally the coach spoke.

"Captain Ruggles, do you and your ten men feel that you are going out there to represent Dulac with credit to Dulac, to yourself, and to your fathers and mothers?"

"Yes," they yelled in chorus.

"All right, then," said the coach. "Let's go."

As Elmer stood out on the field, catching now and then one of the long twisting spirals which Jones sent down the field, he thought, between kicks, how much more effective had been that silence and those few words of Coach Brown's, than the lengthy tirades delivered by his old high school coach, Smith, or such "oratorical eloquence" as Windy Bill and his friends had wished to indulge in. Everything that could be done, had been done during the week, and if it hadn't been done, it was too late, fifteen minutes before the game, to do it. The whole point was, the Dulac team was mentally fit for a real contest, and the coach had said nothing to upset this status. A barrage of oratorical emotionalism by Lou Harmonica, or any of the other alumni, would have ruined them. Elmer appreciated for the first time the trials and tribulations to which a college coach is subject, and still more he appreciated the fact that the Dulac coach was preeminently a man of sound common sense.

Rip won the toss and chose to take the wind. The Aksarben captain elected to kick off. The game was beginning.

The eleven men all shook hands before they went out, and as they lined up to receive, Elmer for the first time took a look around the field. Every available seat was taken and both stands were a riot of color, noise and music. He heard faintly the "Fight, fight, fight!" coming as a chant from the Dulac sections, while from the Aksarben sections, even more faintly, he heard the words of their state song, "We're from Aksarben." He was surprised to find how cool and collected he was and how his every faculty was at his command. That full year's experience, two years previous, had done its fruitful work.

"Are you ready, Captain Ruggles?" called the referee. "Are you ready, Captain Bay?"

The whistle sounded and an instant later Lord, the giant Aksarben halfback, had sent the ball soaring far over the goal line. The great game was begun.

Jones went back and fell on the ball for a touchback. The ball was brought out to the twenty yard line. Instead of calling for the customary punt formation, Elmer called for "Close formation A, right, 82, 98, 46, 15, hip," and the backfield shifted to the right. Elmer faked the ball to Jones who went through all the motions of a line plunge — but Jones didn't have the ball. Elmer still held it. Running straight back, with his back to the other team, Elmer suddenly whirled and threw the ball diagonally over his left shoulder; forty yards across the field the ball traveled, just far enough and just high enough so that Kerr, the left end, running full speed down the field, was able to reach it.

He bobbled it for an instant, but finally tucked it away; then, on and on, straight down the field, he continued, not being tackled until, just as he crossed the goal line, the Aksarben safety man lunged for him. Elmer went jogging down the field with the rest of the team and found the referee carrying the ball out to the five yard line.

"Place kick formation," called Elmer, "89, 49, 56, 15;" and instantly the ball was snapped back to Elmer who, resting on his left knee, placed it straight up and down on the ground alongside of him, holding it in place with the index finger of his right hand. A fraction of a second later, Jones sent the ball sailing between the goal posts for the extra point. The score was seven to nothing. The crowd had not had time to realize what had happened.

As the team which has a touchdown scored against it has the choice, the Aksarben captain chose to receive. Jones kicked off for Dulac, sending the ball high in the air to the Aksarben fullback. The Aksarben fullback was extremely slow in getting started and was tackled on his own fifteen yard line. Aksarben, finding itself unable to gain on the first two plays, kicked on the third down to midfield. Elmer was back there to receive the punt, but when he saw both Aksarben ends right on top of him, ready to tackle him, he signaled for a fair catch.

"That's the old head work!" said Credon, running up.

An instant later, they lined up. "This is a Dulac year," yelled Rip. "Come on, boys, let's show them what we're made of."

"84, 38, 29, 52," called Elmer. This time the backfield shifted to the left, Elmer got the ball from the center, and went through all the motions, facial and otherwise, that would indicate his intention to again throw a pass to Kerr; although Kerr, this time, was well covered by the fleet Lord. Elmer faked the pass to Kerr, stopped it with his left hand, and threw the ball short, right into the arms of the right end who had cut across into the territory vacated by Lord. Ten yards he traveled, after catching the ball, before he was tackled by another Aksarben back. Aksarben took time out. It was apparent that they were panicky; quite demoralized for the time being.

The two minutes allowed for time out being up, both teams lined up again. It was first down ten for Dulac. Again Elmer called a series of numbers that shifted his players to the right. Faking as though he had the ball, Elmer was running wide and an instant later, Jones, the fullback, went crashing through center for twelve yards. The Aksarben defensive center had pulled out, leaving his position undefended. It was first down on Aksarben's twenty yard line.

On the next play the team again shifted to the right and again Elmer went streaking out to the right. This time nobody watched him, or followed him; and in another instant, Credon, who had received the ball from the center, placed a beautiful pass into Elmer's arms and in two steps he was across the goal line for the second touchdown.

Jones again kicked goal, making the score fourteen to nothing. The Aksarben team again chose to receive, but being deep in their own territory, were unable to gain. Dulac scored two more touchdowns that half, though there were no more forward passes thrown. The Aksarben team had gone to pieces completely; they seemed hopelessly outclassed from then on; they had never, from the very beginning, been in a position where they could exert their full offensive strength. Elmer had outguessed them at every turn, and the third and fourth touchdowns were the result of beautiful parades down the field.

The second half was a repetition of the first, except that Aksarben fought harder and with more cohesion. They stopped Dulac twice when touchdowns appeared imminent, and in the fourth quarter launched a beautiful offensive, headed by the giant Lord, which yielded them one touchdown. When the gun went off at the end of the game the score stood thirty-four to seven in favor of Dulac. The Aksarben team had fought doggedly and tenaciously, but except for the last five or six minutes they lacked that exhilaration and enthusiasm which is so essential to success.

An instant later the crowd swept out on the field and it was with some difficulty that Elmer made his way out, and over to the gymnasium. To his surprise he felt no particular emotional joy in the victory; just a keen sense of satisfaction. Everyone seemed to be happy, but happy with restraint.

"South Square and Kingston haven't got much this year," announced Rip to the boys in the shower baths, "but I don't think we have much of a chance to win from that State team."

"We'll win from State," said Elmer, "or they'll have to come out and carry my dead body off the field."

A student manager just then came in hunting for Rip and Elmer. "Coach Brown wants you and Higgins to come into his office."

Entering the coach's office a minute later with Rip, Elmer saw that the room was filled with the same group of alumni that had been in the dressing room before the game. They were noisy, filled with enthusiasm, singing college songs, and slapping one another and Coach Brown on the back, though the coach, to Elmer's eye, was plainly bored. He gave Rip and Elmer a sly, good-humored look as they came in.

"I congratulate you, boys!" exclaimed Windy Bill, as he spied Elmer and Rip entering. "The greatest game of football ever played by any team anywhere! Ruggles, as a guard, you are magnificent, and Higgins, your strategy was superb, immense. And we have the best little coach there is in the business. Anybody that ever criticizes Coach Brown will have to reckon with me. The way he planned that game today ought to satisfy anybody. It was the greatest piece of strategy I ever saw."

When Elmer and Rip, after a minute or two of this, turned and went out, the last sound they heard was Windy Bill's voice still rolling out its noisy praises of coach and team.

As they stood on the steps of the gym, Rip shook Elmer by the hand. "Boy, you have sure come back!"

"Thanks a lot, Rip," said Elmer, "but I won't be satisfied till we've beaten State."

CHAPTER

17

RIVALS

Elmer was late in arriving at the hotel where the dance was being held. The rush at the tailor's had delayed the delivery of his tuxedo to such an extent that Rip had to go ahead in a cab, and take the girls to the ballroom. Elmer was to join them there as soon as he could. He was still further delayed by the fact that it took him over a half hour to tie his dress tie. Rip had always previously performed this ritual. However, at last he had his studs properly adjusted and the tie smoothed out so that it satisfied his critical eye.

The dance was already in full swing when Elmer arrived. It was a formal party, and a very expensive orchestra had been imported from Chicago. Checking his hat and overcoat, Elmer had no more than entered the ballroom when he was surrounded by at least a dozen persons, all wishing to congratulate him on the game of the afternoon. Visibly embarrassed by these attentions, Elmer could do nothing except stand there and discuss the various points of the game with the crowd, and answer divers questions; and all the time he grew more and more nervously anxious to join his own group. Finally he spied Rip and the two girls standing together at one side. He excused himself from the crowd, and immediately went over to them.

"I thought you were going to give us the ritz," Ruth laughed. "Now that you're so famous, I didn't know whether you'd care to come over and associate with common people."

"Were you waiting here long? I'm awfully sorry," Elmer answered. "Really, I broke away just as soon as I could."

"It was certainly thrilling this afternoon," said Estelle. "I was never so surprised in my life as when I saw you out there playing quarterback."

"Yes," continued Ruth, "you might at least have given us a hint or something, — we wouldn't have told anybody."

"Well, we gave our word to the coach," said Rip, "and I know you wouldn't want us to break our word, would you?"

"I think it was wonderful," said Estelle, "and all the more wonderful because it was such a surprise."

At that instant the orchestra struck up one of the prevalent "blues" and both boys immediately took out their programs, to see what arrangements they had made for exchanging dances.

"Rip," said Ruth, "we've got to save a few dances for the two young men who took us to the game this afternoon."

"Oh, you mean Joe College and Dan Dormitory — are they here tonight?"

"Now, Rip, I think it's perfectly outrageous for you to try to ridicule those two boys. They were kind enough to take us to the game this afternoon, and they're very nice boys, too."

"Of course, they're nice!" laughed Rip, "and, of course, we'll save these men all the dances which you think they may want." But there was mischief in his eyes as he spoke.

"I believe this is our dance, Estelle," interpolated Elmer, and excusing himself, he and Estelle swung off across the floor.

There was a gay crowd at the dance, and an atmosphere of brightness and relaxation that made Elmer feel that he was on top of the world as he glided around the floor with his charming partner. That number finished, the four of them were again standing together in the same corner.

Suddenly, "Here come the two anecdotes," whispered Rip to Elmer, as two young men sauntered across the floor towards them. "No funny stuff, now," said Elmer, "remember, try to be a gentleman."

The two young men were effusive in their greetings to the girls, and on being introduced to Rip and Elmer were painfully polite. Their real names proved to be Filbert Magg and Maurice Day.

"A ripping game you played this afternoon," ventured Filbert.

"Thank you," said Rip, "very glad you enjoyed it."

"Quite interesting," volunteered Maurice. "It's rather seldom that I enthuse, but I must say this afternoon was an exception."

"Very nice of you to say so," replied Elmer.

"Are you gentlemen stagging it tonight?" asked Rip.

"Yes," replied Filbert, "and we're having a jolly time."

"Well, here are our programs," volunteered Rip, taking his and Elmer's and proffering them to the boys. "Fill in what you wish, as I know it is the ladies' pleasure."

Elmer noticed the flicker of a smile creeping around the corner of Rip's mouth, and he was so afraid that at any time Rip might "say something" in his usual unexpected style, that he decided it might be best to break up the conversation until later on. He turned to Messrs. Filbert and Maurice.

"When the intermission comes won't the two of you join us, while we go out on the mezzanine?" he asked.

"We should be very happy to." The answers came so nearly like a chorus that Rip nearly laughed. Anyway, the "twins" were rid of for a while.

Elmer danced the next dance with Ruth.

"I believe I'm going to like your two friends," said Elmer, trying to draw Ruth on.

"I think they're perfectly all right," returned Ruth. "I know Rip doesn't like them at all, and I felt sure he would say something that would hurt their feelings."

"Hurt their feelings? Oh, no, — why should he do that?"

But Ruth merely gave him a sly look, and said nothing.

The evening was passing very pleasantly and swiftly. In no time at all, it seemed, came the intermission. The six of them moved out to the mezzanine, and seated at a large table were presently served with ices; and then the fun began for Rip, and Elmer, saying nothing but listening to the conversation of the two "staggers."

"How do you like your new Stutz roadster?" said Filbert to Maurice.

"Oh, I don't know; I haven't been able to get more than sixty-five out of it so far," replied that airy young gentleman. "You know," he explained, turning to the girls, "father promised me a fast car for going on that frumpy yacht trip this summer — always such a bore to me — and I was a little bit disappointed when he gave me the Stutz."

"I smashed up the family Cunningham last summer, up in the woods, and the family won't let me have a car now for a whole year," Maurice complained.

The girls looked at Rip, and Elmer looked at Rip, but that young gentleman displayed an inscrutable countenance; his manner indicated only the most polite interest. Maurice made some more remarks to the effect that he would have to join the folks down in Florida during the Christmas holidays. Filbert's remarks were something to the effect that possibly he might not return to school the second half as he might have to go with his people to Europe. But no matter what was said Elmer and Rip still remained scrupulously attentive. And as the game played on, the girls grew plainly more and more ill at ease. They tried, time and again, unsuccessfully, to swerve the conversation over to football.

Shortly after the intermission, Elmer and Rip took the girls home; their families did not permit them to keep the usual midnight-and-after hours of dancing parties.

"Well, I suppose Maurice will take you to the dance next Saturday night," said Elmer to Estelle, as they drove along in the taxi.

"He may," Estelle answered, "but really I'm afraid he isn't the gentleman I thought he was."

"Why, I think he's a perfect gentleman," said Elmer.

"A gentleman doesn't make other people envious by telling them about all the good things he has in life."

"Under that definition your friend is still a gentleman," replied Elmer, "because I can assure you that he didn't arouse any trace of envy so far as I am concerned."

"Well, I was disappointed," Estelle admitted frankly. "He was so nice at the game."

"Isn't he still nice — nicer than I am?" asked Elmer, as the cab stopped in front of her door.

But Estelle only laughed, and called out "Good night" as she ran up the walk to her door.

The following week end the Varsity, twenty-four strong, went down and beat the ancient and honorable foe, South Square, fourteen to nothing. Elmer played almost the entire game at quarterback, though he did no spectacular playing. The game was really won by the spectacular off-tackle dashes of Credon and Miller. South Square's attack was powerful, and they were able to gain quite a bit of ground in the middle of the field. However, Dulac stopped them whenever they became dangerous.

The team arrived home the Monday morning after the game. That afternoon they began active preparations for the Kingston game at home, the following Saturday. Kingston, however, was reported to be weak, and Coach Brown instructed the quarterbacks to try to win the game without throwing a single forward pass. However, there was no let up in the forward pass practice during the week. Perfection in the execution of the pass was the one thing above all others aimed at daily, the coach having in mind the State game, the last game of the year, as a climax to the season. The coach, in fact, continually kept drumming into the ears of the boys the State game, while he apparently paid but little attention to the game the coming Saturday; and this, of course, kept Elmer keyed to pitch, for to him the State game, and victory over Smith, was the be-all and end-all of the season.

After dinner at the Fellowship Club Friday evening, Rip motioned Elmer to a chair alongside him.

"Something has happened to our friends, Joe and Dan," said Rip. "The girls are going to the game tomorrow with Ruth's mother. Something has happened, but I haven't heard what it is. We're both invited up to Ruth's house tomorrow night for dinner. We may and we may not hear what has happened to our two friends. I'm inclined to believe that they talked themselves out of the league."

"I had a letter from home today," said Elmer, changing the subject, "and my folks are going to be down for the State game."

"Yes," said Elmer, "and the folks are going. Mother writes that father is all het up over football, and has his chest out so you can't touch him with a ten-foot pole."

"It certainly makes a difference, when his boy is playing quarterback," laughed Rip.

"Oh, keep quiet," said Elmer, "but I sure am glad to see the old gentleman changing around. He certainly was strong the other way for a long time."

"My father was just the opposite," said Rip. "I know he would have been keenly disappointed if I hadn't made the team. In fact, in high school, I don't believe I would have gone out at all, but for his encouragement."

They were interrupted then by Professor Noon, who strode over and challenged Elmer to a game of chess. This was a favorite diversion of the old professor, and he was more than a match for anyone in the club.

"How is it you're not going out to the Country Club tonight?" he asked Elmer during the course of their game.

"It's a little late in the year," said Elmer, "and besides I don't believe the coach is taking the game tomorrow quite as seriously as he might. We're quietly spending most of our time preparing for the State game."

"We have a surprisingly good team this year," said Professor Noon, "but I don't believe we have much chance against State. They seem to be running rough shod over all their opponents, and with very little difficulty."

Elmer's eyes flashed and his jaw set, but he said nothing further.

The game against Kingston proved a great deal more difficult than was expected. Kingston displayed its traditional aggressiveness which for a time completely neutralized the speed and cunning of the Dulac team. However, in the third quarter the Dulac team marched fifty yards to the eighteen yard line, from which point Miller scored on one of his eel-like runs. The final score, seven to nothing, was rather disappointing to the Dulac adherents, who packed the stands, but the coaches and the players themselves were entirely satisfied.

"It may not look so good," said Elmer to Rip in the dressing room after the game, "but, anyway, we didn't have to show anything. We have at least a dozen plays which the State scouts have never seen, and if they work as well in the game as they have in practice, we'll give Coach Smith the surprise of his life."

"Coach Smith," said Rip, winking to his roommate, "who is he? Is he the fellow who coaches State?"

"Don't try to be funny," said Elmer, "the State game is one thing that I'm serious about."

The dinner at Ruth's home that night was the good old-fashioned family kind. Mrs. Fife was a motherly soul who took such pride and satisfaction in preparing a real meal, that both Elmer and Rip had a hard time to keep from eating more than was proper.

"I don't know much about this game of football," said Mrs. Fife, "but I sure do enjoy watching the cheer leader."

"Oh, mother, don't you think that Rip and Elmer played a wonderful game?"

"Oh, my yes," said her mother. "They were just grand, but I did enjoy watching that cheer leader turn somersaults. All his antics are so interesting."

Rip and Elmer enjoyed that.

"Don't you think, Mrs. Fife, that you could get away and come down and see the State game?"

"Oh, my, no," she replied, "my husband would think there was something wrong with my mind!"

"Where were your friends this afternoon?" asked Rip later that evening, during a pause in the music. "I don't think it was very gallant of them to let you girls go to the game with your mother alone."

Elmer noticed a little rising color in Estelle's cheeks, but she ventured no reply.

"What a great pair of heroes they'd be in case our country were at war," Rip went on banteringly. "I imagine both of them would qualify very nicely for a job delivering telegrams in Washington, D. C."

"I think it's horrid of you, Rip, to be making remarks like that," said Ruth. "They may have their faults, but they are fine boys."

"Admitting that they might be 'fine boys,'" parried Rip, "what might their faults be?"

"Oh, don't make out that you don't know," said Ruth. "You know as well as I do that Filbert Magg's father is just an ordinary practicing physician in Detroit, and Maurice Day's father is in the butter and egg business in Cincinnati. They like to pretend a bit, but they don't mean any harm."

"Fourflush, you mean," said Rip.

"Now, Rip, it isn't nice of you to talk like that."

"Well, I believe in speaking frankly," said Rip. "What you have said has been all news to me, but I will say this, it was very welcome news."

"Oh, is that so," laughed Ruth, but she was plainly growing self-conscious in the face of Rip's outright talking.

The situation, however, was relieved, as Ruth's mother came along at this moment and entered the circle.

Rip and Elmer left an hour later, both in high spirits. "What's the idea of these fellows trying to put this bonton stuff over on us? I thought they were exaggerating a little the other night when they were talking about yachts and all that sort of rot, but I didn't think they were just a pair of bold-faced liars."

"As Ruth said," replied Elmer, "they were just pretending. But what's the harm, since the girls have seen through them?"

"Yes, they must have got the air, all right. But if they bother the girls again they'll get more than that from me."

"Now, remember, sonny, you must always be a gentleman," Elmer cautioned in a paternal way.

"Well, I mean it!" said Rip; then he paused for a moment and thought. "You're right; there's no use paying any more attention to those chaps — we'll forget them."

Two things ran through Elmer's mind that night. One of them was the impending game with State, now three weeks off; he knew within himself that his football efforts so far were trivial compared with the efforts he would put forth in that game. His other thought was of Estelle. Her coolness and indifference provoked him. It was two o'clock before he fell asleep.

CHAPTER
18

A SCOUTING TRIP

The following Friday afternoon, as Elmer stepped into the locker room preparatory to dressing for practice, he was met by one of the student managers.

"The coach wants to see you in his office."

Wondering what was up, Elmer hurried back and entered the coach's room. He found Rip and Jones already there.

"What's up?" inquired Elmer.

"We don't know any more than you do, but the coach will be back in a minute."

A few minutes later in strode the coach. He busied himself about his desk for a minute, after having greeted the boys. Then he turned to them.

"This Hochtel game tomorrow doesn't amount to much, and we would possibly win it with our third team, if necessary, so I have suddenly decided that the three of you and I will go down and look over State's game tomorrow."

Elmer's heart fairly jumped.

"They are playing Tecumseh," the coach continued. "Tecumseh has a real good team and ought to give them at least a fair contest. Of course, our scouts have seen every game State has played so far this year, and we have accurate information on their offense and defense, but I believe we can learn a little more. So far, their defense appears impregnable and their offense almost irresistible. So it will be up to the four of us to see if we can't find some weak spot in their play which we can take advantage of when our game comes.

We have a half hour to catch the train, so hurry up, pack your bags, and meet me at the station."

The boys quickly dispersed. Elmer and Rip hurried to their rooms and in five minutes had their bags packed and were swinging down the avenue towards the station.

"I certainly am glad the coach picked me to go along," said Rip. "It has been so long since I've seen a game I won't know what to look for."

"It sure was a welcome surprise to me, too," said Elmer. "I can hardly wait to see what kind of a defensive game State plays. They must be vulnerable to some kind of an attack."

"I wonder where we will sit," said Rip.

"Presumably in the press box," replied Elmer. "Coach Brown has probably wired to State for tickets up there."

About a block from the station they encountered two of the students who were also members of the Fellowship Club. One of them was the editor of the Daily, and the other the manager of the Glee Club.

"Where are you two going?" asked one of them. "Haven't we got a game here tomorrow?"

"Yes," replied Rip, "but Coach Brown is taking three of us down to see the State game tomorrow."

"Huh, I wonder if I can say anything about that in the Daily?"

"You'd better come down to the station and see the coach," replied Rip; "that would be the safest thing to do."

Coach Brown was in front of the ticket agent's window, purchasing the tickets, when the boys arrived at the station.

"I understand that you and three of the players are going down to State tomorrow to scout," said the Daily editor. "Do you mind if I run that story in the Daily tomorrow morning?"

"Not at all," said Coach Brown, turning around to see who it was talking. "I've already wired Coach Smith at State that we are coming, and asked for seats in the press box. There's nothing at all mysterious about this scouting; it's all open and above board. We're going down to see just how strong State is — to look over their strength, and to discover, if possible, any weaknesses. State will have two scouts up here tomorrow, though in a game such as we will play against Hochtel they won't see very much."

Just then the train pulled in, and the four Dulac men, coach and players, boarded the chair car.

"We could have ridden up in the day coach," Brown remarked as he relaxed in the big soft spacious Pullman seat, "but it's a long five-hour run to State and there's no use tiring ourselves unnecessarily. We'll make ourselves as comfortable as we can here; we can go back into the diner about six.

"We might as well talk over some of the details of what we are going to do tomorrow right now," continued Coach Brown. "After dinner we may be too full of food to think clearly and tomorrow morning we may not have time for any detailed talk. When State has the ball I want you, Rip, to watch the offensive line play. I have here a pair of field glasses which I'll loan you. Focus these on the individual men and see if you can detect any weakness in their stance or in the secondary reaction of their charge. If you have any line men pulling out to run interference in any of their plays let me know at once, and also how they go out.

"Elmer, on offense I want you to make notes on what plays they use in the various parts of the field, under the varying conditions, so that you can get a definite idea of their tactics and strategy.

"Jones, I want you to watch how their interference works. Sometimes they use straight line interference and other times they use the echelon type. Watch closely and see if there are any signs by which you can tell ahead of time which type of interference they will use. Also watch the ball carriers, and see if they have any peculiarities of any sort.

"I will be watching everything in general myself, checking up on their plays, particularly their forward pass plays. When State is on defense I want you, Rip, to watch the guards and tackles the same as you watch the line on offense. Jones, I want you to concentrate on the center and fullback and see how they play under the varying conditions. Elmer, I want you to watch particularly their defense against forward passes. I understand they use the strict zone defense and I want to verify this. Also check up and see just where the various backs and the center are when Tecumseh executes a forward pass. I'll watch their ends myself and also their varying defensive formations.

"I hope Tecumseh is strong enough on offense so that we can get a good line on State's defense, and I also hope that Tecumseh is weak on defense so that State's offense will function smoothly. If State's offense does function smoothly it will be much easier for us to find the various things we are looking for.

"From what I have been able to gather," continued Coach Brown, "our only chance lies in being able to forward pass them. From all reports we have received, they have a wonderful line, wonderfully coached by the assistant coach down there, a man named Green. The four backs are all natural football men, athletes who do the right thing more by natural instinct than because they have been told. However, a team is no stronger than its line. It's that wonderful line of theirs which accounts for most of their success. Behind a weak line no backs would ever have a chance to get started. A powerful line can make an ordinary back look like a star."

"Might it not be possible that they will use a different defense against us than they will use against Tecumseh?" inquired Elmer.

"Yes, that's quite likely. It is quite likely that they will change their formations on defense, but their personnel can't change. It's personnel and individual proficiency that we'll be analyzing tomorrow, to a large extent."

After dinner they called for a table, which was brought to them by the Pullman porter, and they played whist the rest of the way. They arrived at State at about nine-thirty that night and went immediately to the hotel. Feeling tired from the rather long ride, Rip and Elmer went up to bed. The next morning Coach Brown called them at seven-thirty with instructions to be down to breakfast at eight-thirty. After breakfast Coach Brown called a taxi and they were driven out to the immense stadium which was situated about a mile from the center of the town. The athletic office of State was situated across the street from the stadium and it was there Coach Brown instructed the taxi driver to pull up.

They found Coach Smith alone in his office. He was apparently busily engaged at a long table which was entirely covered with newspaper clippings.

"How are you, Mr. Brown? We feel highly honored to have you pay us a visit."

"Thank you," replied the Dulac coach, "we just thought we would come up here and see if we could find out how you do it."

Coach Brown then introduced the others, and when Coach Smith shook hands with Elmer, he remarked, turning to Coach Brown, "So you made a quarterback of my young friend here from Springfield — you are certainly to be congratulated. By the way, before I forget about it, here are your four seats in the press box for this afternoon."

"Do you mind if the four of us go over to your stadium this morning and look over your field?" asked Brown. "You certainly have a wonderful edifice there and if you don't mind we would enjoy looking around a bit."

"Certainly! I'll send one of my assistants over with you to let you in, and show you around. I would go with you myself, only — you see! Busy! busy! Too much work!"

"Publicity?" Brown inquired, glancing at the newspaper clippings covering the desk.

"Yes; I've made several speeches in several of the big cities near here, and the talks have attracted quite a bit of attention in the papers. You'll see here I have clippings from papers from coast to coast, reporting about them. I certainly made some fine statements, particularly along the line of athletics, and these clippings here don't begin to do me justice."

"I've heard you could go on a chautauqua any time," said Coach Brown. "If you should quit coaching you wouldn't have to worry about a livelihood."

"Well, there are a lot of people who have the wrong impression on a lot of things, and it's up to some of us to correct them," Coach Smith said, with a gesture.

"You certainly had nice success with your team this year."

"Yes, I feel very gratified," replied Coach Smith. "I took a lot of green boys two years ago, and they have developed so you would hardly know them today."

"Do you have much assistance in your coaching?" inquired Coach Brown.

"Not any to speak of. I have a couple of men who just carry out my orders as best they can, but the brunt of the work falls on me individually. But you have to know how to handle men, you know, to get the best results out of them."

"Well, we must be going," said Coach Brown. "If I have time I hope I can see you for about a minute after the game."

"Fine," replied Coach Smith, "I'll look for you. And if there's anything we can do to make you more comfortable when you come down in two weeks, please feel free to call on us. Goodbye, Mr. Brown; goodbye, boys; it's very nice of you to come up here to see me. By the way, Higgins, when you are down looking over the stadium, you will find that it has a real high fence all around it."

As they went down the steps, Rip turned to Elmer. "What the deuce did he mean by that last crack of his?"

"I guess he means that when the game starts, I'll try to run out of the park, but the fence will be too high — but I'll fool him, the conceited donkey. Did you ever see a man who loved himself like he does?"

"He does use the first person now and then," Rip replied smiling; "but then, of course, he may have a right to."

"Oh, shucks," Elmer answered, "from what I've heard, Green, his assistant coach, does most of the real coaching, and Smith does the handshaking. It'll be interesting to hear the alibis he'll have to offer after we beat them."

The stadium proved to be beautifully arranged. Every seat was evidently a good point of vantage from which to watch the game. The facilities for handling the crowd were well taken care of in every way; but what impressed Elmer most of all was the wonderful quality of the turf — the resiliency and toughness of it. It was as smooth as a carpet, and it was evident, even to his inexperienced eye, that the field would be fast unless there was an exceptionally heavy rain.

"This is certainly a wonderful stadium" Rip exclaimed.

"Yes, but I bet it's worrying somebody about who's going to pay for it. The interest and overhead on a place of this sort must be tremendous. How about those air-currents we've read about?" Elmer inquired of Coach Brown.

"Don't worry about any air-currents," the coach replied. "They're all a myth. You'll catch a punt here just exactly as you would back home."

A quarter of two that afternoon found all four of the Dulac men nicely located in the press box. At their end of the enclosure there were several scouts from another school who were there to look over the Tecumseh team. The other end of the press box was occupied entirely by sports writers. Alongside of each sports writer was a Western Union operator, with an instrument at his elbow. The clatter and the noise of the instruments during the game were confusing to one not used to them. Elmer turned his attention to the field.

The usual preliminaries over, the two captains met in the middle of the field with the officials, and a few minutes later Tecumseh kicked off to State. The game was just about as Coach Brown had hoped it would be. Tecumseh was powerful on offense, but weak on defense. However, powerful as Tecumseh was it was unable to score, while the wonderful State team ran up a grand total of thirty-five points during the course of the afternoon.

Paying no attention to the ball, or to the game in general, Elmer found himself engrossed with the task at hand. He had four sheets of paper, each one representing a diagram of the field. He used one of these for each quarter. He charted the game for each quarter, and, alongside of each down, he put the kind of play which the State quarterback used. When Tecumseh had the ball, Elmer concentrated on State's defense against the forward pass, and found that they were using the zone defense. It was quite effective that afternoon. However, Elmer could readily see that this was due both to the individual proficiency of the men in State's backfield, and to the lack of deception in Tecumseh's forward passing attack. The game was drawn out much longer than had been expected; and so, immediately after the game, without again seeing the State coach, Coach Brown called a cab and they hurried to the station just in time to catch their train home.

Elmer was surprised to find that, despite his inactivity, he had a keen appetite.

"Immediately after dinner," announced Coach Brown, "we'll spend one-half hour completing our notes, then we'll get together for a conference."

The conference, however, failed to produce the results expected.

"If there are any weak spots in that line, offensively or defensively, I failed to find them," said Rip. "I never saw such a line for cohesiveness, leg drive, and sustained power. It looks as if the forward pass will be our only chance. They use the wedge line almost entirely on offensive, but they had such perfection of execution that they just lifted the Tecumseh line out of the way."

"To be perfectly honest," said Jones, "I didn't see very much. If they use both the straight line and the staggered type of interference, I couldn't distinguish between them. Their fullback, Renfrew, on defense is the best I've ever seen. Their defensive center stayed on the line all afternoon, but Renfrew seemed to have a wonderful nose for plays. He was up close on line plays and he was back against forward passes."

"What did you notice, Higgins?" asked the coach.

"Well, my notes show that today their tactics and strategy are absolutely orthodox. Inside their own twenty yard line they kick on first down and then up nearer to the middle of the field they kick on third down. They throw no forward passes in their own territory. In fact they play very cut-and-dried zone football. They'll never surprise the defense, as far as I can see. Their defense against passes is the zone type. Tecumseh's passes, however, were so simple that they were never tested. Renfrew, their fullback, comes up awfully fast on line plunges, and it's my opinion that a fake line plunge followed by a forward pass will fool him.

"Good!" the coach commented enthusiastically "Now, is there anything about their offense that you noticed which might be of value or interest?"

"Just this," replied Elmer, "and I noticed it late in the second half — their quarterback leads every play except their fake reverse play."

"Very good. Our other scouts have brought back that point, too, and I paid particular attention to it today to verify it. I believe that is a point which will prove a valuable asset to us. Their quarterback does lead every play except the fake reverse play."

"What do you mean by a fake 'reverse play,'" inquired Rip, "if you'll pardon my ignorance?"

"Well, I'll explain it," said the coach. "A reverse play is where the back behind center gets the ball, fakes off-tackle, and then passes the ball back to another back, generally the outside back, who runs around the opposite end. Some people call it a criss-cross play. Now, on that play the quarterback headed the interference back toward the opposite end. However, in the fake reverse play, the halfback who gets the ball from the center fakes off-tackle and then acts as if he passes the ball back to the halfback the same as he did on the reverse play. However, he hangs on to the ball and spins back through the line. Our defensive tackles can stop the fake reverse play if they get enough practice on it. Our defensive full and center, by watching the offensive quarter, should be in on every play. With our team thoroughly trained on that point, I'm certain we can stop them; but I will say that I've never seen a team with such power and speed. Personally, I have come to the conclusion that Jones can hold his own with Hunk Hughes in kicking, and I therefore believe we'd better try a kicking game and play for the breaks. If there are any fumbles we *must* get the ball. It's useless to think of trying to make any kind of a march against that kind of a team, and forward passing against them appears to be dangerous.

"However, I agree with you, Elmer, that a fake line plunge, followed by a forward pass up the middle of the field, looks like our best bet. Renfrew does come forward a little too fast to be able to stop that kind of a forward pass. However, he won't be susceptible to that kind of a pass very often, and you'd better save that play for a time when it will do the most good.

"That line of theirs is wonderfully coached; for all practical purposes it will be impregnable to our rushing attack. However, you, Jones, will have to crash in through that line for some gains. If you can make a few gains successfully it will bring Renfrew up closer, thus giving our forward pass plays a much better chance.

"There was no general weakness on defense that I could see outside of these points. Their quarterback handles the punts remarkably well, though he is not particularly adept at returning them. Our plan will have to be a strong kicking game with every man alert for a fumble. If we can get the ball up deep in their territory, we will have to score either by means of a forward pass or a place kick by Jones."

They discussed the game until about eleven o'clock, when the porter announced that they were pulling into Dulac.

CHAPTER
19

THE SCENE OF BATTLE

Monday noon Coach Brown began his work with the team by congratulating them on playing good football in defeating Hochtel the previous Saturday.

"I'm sorry I couldn't have been here to see it, but the coaching staff tells me there was marked improvement in the play all along the line. Jones, Captain Ruggles, Higgins, and myself went down and saw State wallop Tecumseh. I want to say right here that State has as fine a football team as I have ever seen. They can hit the line, they can run the ends, they can forward pass, and their kicking game is strong.

"They have no weakness whatsoever on defense. They don't fumble and they are alert. They have wonderful aggressiveness, perfect morale, and they are going to play us on their own field — don't forget that! When they open up that line attack of theirs, driving those fast starting, crashing backs behind that powerful line, they may go through us five and ten yards at a play; whereas our attack, when it hits those tackles of theirs, may break like waves hitting a rockbound shore.

"And yet, I think we can beat them. We are Dulac. We are representing an institution with personality and soul, with almost a century of time-honored tradition. I have confidence in every one of the men here, and I believe we can rise to heights because of this glorious background behind us. Whereas, State has become such a large school, such a tremendous proposition, that it has almost lost its personality and soul, and most of its traditions have been forgotten. And I believe that when we go out there, man to man, where nothing else counts but sheer grit, pluck, aggressiveness, mental and physical alertness and control, I believe that you boys will prove their masters.

"The margin of difference between victory and defeat is very slight. I want every man to take complete notes on the defense I have planned against State — and I am also going to add two plays to our repertoire. These plays are very similar to the ones we already have, except that in their denouement there is an element of surprise. I am not any particular disciple of Coué, but I do believe that if we keep repeating to ourselves, for the next two weeks, 'we will win, we must win, we can win,' that it will bolster up our determination and put backbone in our *will* to win."

There was no scrimmage work at all during the week. Two or three of the players who were still suffering from the effects of the Kingston game and one or two suffering from injuries in the Hochtel game, were rounding into shape nicely.

"The coach says we may get a few minutes on defense and offense next week, just to keep our judgment of timing and distance on edge and to tune us up for the game," said Rip, when he and Elmer were discussing the situation. "He says there will be no more grueling scrimmage, as he's going to take absolutely no chance on any injuries. He said he'd rather have, the team a little under-scrimmaged, but chuck full of enthusiasm and vim, than to have them over-scrimmaged, which means they would be a little dull and listless the day of the game."

"I like to scrimmage, though," said Elmer.

"There's nothing I like better, either," replied Rip, "but the coach has probably weighed all the values and with his experience he no doubt knows what is best."

The team eased up in its work on Friday. All during the week Elmer had practiced over and over again that one particular play in which he faked the ball to Jones on a line plunge and then running back passed it to Kerr, the left end, who would cut in towards the middle. The execution was nearing perfection. On Friday, however, the work consisted entirely of kicking and covering punts. Jones was punting better than at any time in his career, and he was lofting them high into the air, the ball sometimes carrying seventy yards before it finally nestled into the arms of some receiver, or hitting the ground went rolling up the field.

The second team played the entire first half the next day against Reliance, scoring one touchdown in that time. At the start of the second half, when the Reliance team found that they were up against the first team of Dulac, their morale cracked and they offered but a sporadic resistance during the rest of the game. Confining themselves to straight football, the first string Varsity rolled up four touchdowns before the end of the game. They were not relieved, but played the entire second half.

"What was the coach's idea in not letting us in until the second half?" inquired Credon of Elmer as they both stood under the same shower bath, soaping themselves down.

"I don't know for sure," said Elmer, "but I believe he has the theory that most of the hard bumps in a football game come in the first fifteen minutes in a game like today's. It was not a question of who would win the game, but there was uneasiness in his mind, probably, on the question of injuries to the regulars. He didn't put us in there until the second half, feeling that by that time the Reliance boys would not be hitting so hard, and hence the dangers of injury would be greatly minimized."

Just then Rip entered the shower rooms and announced that the coach requested that every man be in bed at ten o'clock every evening until after the State game.

"I 'phoned the girls, and called off the dance engagement for tonight," he said, turning to Elmer. "They were real good sports about it. But I've made an engagement for us to go to the first show at the Palace, which lets out at nine o'clock, so we can get back to our room easily before ten."

"That suits me," said Elmer.

The picture at the Palace proved rather uninteresting to Elmer, and he was glad to get out at its conclusion, which came shortly before nine o'clock. Ten minutes' walk brought them to Ruth's home.

"Won't you boys stop in just for a minute?" asked Ruth.

"Thank you," said Rip, "we can, but just for a minute. I'd be a poor captain to break the rule which I am supposed to see enforced."

"I have a little surprise for you," said Ruth, as they sat in the parlor chatting. "Mother and I are going down to the game next Saturday, and I'm trying to persuade Estelle to come along, too."

"Oh, you must come," said Rip, turning to Estelle.

"Well, I don't know," Estelle replied. "Mother doesn't think it quite proper for me to go running away down there, just for a football game; she isn't well enough to go along herself."

"I wish you'd change your mind and come," said Elmer. "My folks will all be there and so will Rip's, and with Ruth and her mother coming the party wouldn't be complete without you."

"Oh, do come," Rip teased. "Come on, Estelle, and I'll arrange to see that you all get tickets in the same location, and after the game is over, since this is the last game of the year, we can all have dinner together. We'll have one big time!"

"I certainly love a good football game," said Estelle, a little wistfully. "I'll let you know next week. I'd love to be with you."

Rip had all the arrangements worked out in his manner before they left.

"Good night, Ruth," he said a few minutes later.

"I'll see you next Saturday after the State game, on the mezzanine of the hotel. I'll send one of the student managers up with your tickets Thursday," and then, turning to Estelle, he continued, "and as for you, little mascot, if you want Dulac to win, you'd better come along. I know Elmer won't be worth a nickel unless he knows you're up there cheering for him."

"Doesn't that sound romantic!" Estelle laughed, "just like a story book, and I used to think you were such a sincere young man."

"Do you think she'll go?" asked Elmer later, as he and Rip were undressing for bed.

"Will she go? Try and keep her away! You're just as unsophisticated regarding girls now as you were two years ago — though I will say you have a suave polished manner that knocks them dead."

"Oh, lay off me! Can't you ever be serious?"

"That's the trouble with you," said Rip, "you're always serious."

"The trouble with you," replied Elmer, "is that you're always too whimsical, but, by George, you'd better be serious next Saturday."

"That's a different story," said Rip. "There's a time and a place for everything."

"All right," said Elmer, "this is the time for sleep; put out the light."

Monday's practice was one of feverish activity. Whereas the team frolicked and played around before the coach's whistle sounded for official practice to begin, after the whistle everything was serious attention and concentration. The team at this time of the season was a unit of one; the boys all liked each other immensely. Whatever bad points they had, they overlooked; they counted only the good points in one another, and as a result, from a psychological point of view, they were a potent organization. They were in a state of mind where all petty jealousies and selfishness were entirely eliminated; — instead there was a feeling of all for one and one for all. It made no difference who carried the ball, the other ten men exerted themselves to the utmost to try to keep from the ball carrier any would-be tacklers. The Dulac team was noted for its effective interference, more than any other one thing.

Tuesday afternoon the Freshmen, using the State plays for ten minutes, were unable to make even a dent in the Varsity defense.

"Just keep watching whichever way the quarterback goes," called Coach Brown, to the center and fullback, "and that will tell you everything. Wherever the State quarterback goes, you go. Our defensive tackle, end and guard can stop their fake reverse. You tackles rush that passer harder. Don't give him time to pick out his man — make him throw hurriedly, and, therefore, inaccurately. Against those passes, you backs cover the man who goes into your zone, until the ball is in the air, then play the ball. Relax all you can so that you can jump high in the air against the forward pass. We're not going to knock down any forward passes next Saturday. When State forward passes, we're going to catch them, except, of course, on fourth down.

"I want every man to keep in mind, constantly, the down and the yards to gain, position on the field, the score, and the time left to play. State will play a very orthodox zone game and you can anticipate in a large measure every play they're going to use. Every man govern himself accordingly. If you halfbacks see the ends start down the field call 'Pass' loud enough to be heard in the next county, so that the other members of the team are warned in time. Don't lisp it out like a timid little girl; bark it out loud, so that everyone can hear you.

"Don't pay any attention to any of their talk on offense. They have a clever bunch, and they may try a little chatter to throw you off your guard. However, as regards the State team, use your eyes only; don't pay any attention to anything they may say.

"Here, you Freshmen, try that spinner play again, where the end goes around and takes the ball from the fullback. When he gets the ball the quarterback leads the interference out around the other end and the center and the fullback should help the end stop the play. When he doesn't get the ball the quarterback doubles up as an extra man on one of our linemen, a very simple thing to diagnose, so when the fullback sprints back into the line with the ball, the guards and the tackles should stop him. If the center and full are watching the quarterback, they should be reinforcing the tackles and guards. Don't be fooled."

And so the work went on for half an hour before the coach announced the end of defense practice for that day.

The Varsity then went on offense, confining itself entirely to a forward passing attack. Although the Freshmen knew that nothing but forward passes were coming, yet Elmer completed many nice passes to Kerr, through sheer individual excellence of performance.

Wednesday they had some work covering kicks and did some tackling in the open. Near the end of the practice the entire squad went in for some live tackling. A half dozen wind sprints completed the workout. Thursday the workout consisted merely of some limbering up exercises; nothing of a serious nature was attempted. Friday morning the entire squad left for State.

The Dulac boys limbered up on State field that afternoon. Elmer was surprised to find that catching punts in the big stadium was just just as easy as catching them back home, exactly as Coach Brown had said it would be. If there were any wind currents present, they never dallied with any of the punts which Jones sent down that afternoon. After the workout the entire squad dressed and were driven out to a nearby country club, where they were to spend the remaining hours before the game.

As they were riding out on the bus Elmer remarked to Rip that he had seen his old druggist friend from Springfield, who had told him that half the town of Springfield would be there on the morrow, coming on a special train.

"I guess they've a complete sell-out," said Rip. "The president of the Senior class told me that every Dulac student had signed up for the special leaving there tomorrow morning. The band was rather peeved because they couldn't come up today, but the faculty refused to allow them to miss any classes. Well, tomorrow at this time it will be all over, and we'll be either heroes or dubs."

"I hope it's heroes," said Elmer. "I hate to spoil Hunk Hughes' great record at State, and I think he is a good enough sport to feel the same way about us; but we must beat Coach Smith. This state wouldn't be big enough to hold him if they win."

"They say the betting odds are two to one on State."

"Oh, this betting stuff gives me a distinct pain," said Elmer. "Some of these pikers when they bet and win, pat themselves on the back and say 'aren't we great fellows?' and if they lose, they sob out loud about it, and want to fire the coach."

Arriving at the Country Club, the boys went to their rooms, after which they came down and partook of a wholesome well-cooked meal. During the dinner a student manager came in.

"There's a crowd of fellows out here from Springfield," he said. "They want to talk to Mr. Higgins."

"Station yourself at the front door," Coach Brown instructed the manager, "and tell everyone, I don't care who it is, that they can't see any of the players until after the game tomorrow. After the game they'll have plenty of time to do all their visiting."

The coach also detailed two other student managers to help out the first one, as it was evident that they were to be busy all evening keeping away visitors and well-wishers.

Immediately after breakfast the next day the team was again loaded into busses and driven into town to the hotel. The coach had reserved the entire top floor of the hotel for the team, and instructed them to take off their shoes and to lie at full length on the bed until the call for lunch. Whereas breakfast had consisted of an orange, a large steak, toast and milk, the luncheon consisted of nothing but consomme with very little toast. After lunch, which was served at eleven o'clock, the team was again instructed to lie at full length on the bed for another hour. At twelve-thirty the phone in each room rang, and the voice of the student manager called, "Everybody downstairs."

The hotel was a maelstrom of excited, jabbering humanity; but, under the leadership of the head student manager, the entire squad made its way to the side door where they were loaded into the bus for the stadium. Arriving at the players' entrance they found there a large crowd, apparently hopeful of being able to sneak into the game some way or another. Each player, in fact, did take in with him one small boy or maybe two, to which the gate keeper made no exception. But that was the end of it. After the student manager had passed the last of the players in, the burly gate keeper slammed the gate. "That's all!" he yelled. "There'll be no gate crashers slipping through here today." Yet, for long afterward, that excited and still hopeful crowd stood jammed around the players' entrance. At every gate it was the same. The scene was set for the battle. The air was electrical with mass excitement. It was unquestionably the greatest sporting event in the history of the Middle West — Dulac and State!

And in the heart of Elmer Higgins, more than any other man on the visiting team, a grim determination to win, to achieve victory!

CHAPTER
20
THE GREAT GAME

"Number twenty-seven," called the student manager.

"Here," replied Elmer, as he walked over and took charge of the sailor bag which the manager picked out of a large trunk.

Slowly and carefully, Elmer began to don his football clothes. He spent a little time adjusting his shoulder pads to just the proper place under the jersey. He was painfully exact as he rolled up his stockings in the football pants with the rubber sponge which went to protect the patella. He re-adjusted the tape around his ankles twice before he felt satisfied. The new shoes which he had broken in the previous week were now snug and comfortable. He squatted down once or twice and feeling that the tape around his thigh guards was a little too tight, loosened the pants, and getting new tape, taped the thigh guards anew. This time they were too loose. Again he experimented, until he felt satisfied that the tape was on tight enough so that it would hold, and not too tight, in which case a sudden tensing might break the tape.

For the first time that year Elmer felt nervous, exceedingly nervous! He shook as he thought of the impending conflict. For an instant that little streak of cowardice which is present in all of us asserted itself. Wouldn't it be better if Mull or Berlin went out there and played today? He felt weak in the pit of his stomach while the thought of his tremendous responsibility overwhelmed him. An instant later his teeth crunched, and his fists clenched, and a rush of blood carried new stiffening to his backbone.

"I've lived a lot preparing for today," said Elmer to himself. "Only a yellow dog would go out there now and quit. I'm just a little bit nervous now, but as soon as the first kick-off is over I'll settle down. Steady, old man, steady! There's a lot depending on you today, and you've got to come through."

He walked over to the fountain in the corner for a drink. He heard voices in the corner.

"I tell you," said one voice, "if you would pull that old shoestring play on the opening play, you would score a touchdown right away."

"That's very kind of you to come in and tell me about this," said the second voice, which Elmer recognized as that of Coach Brown, "but I'm afraid a play of this sort wouldn't work against a veteran team like State."

"Oh, the stupidity of you football coaches makes me sick!" the first voice now exclaimed. "I saw Osceola high pull the shoestring play against Niles, and it was the most beautiful thing you ever saw. If you don't pull it on State this afternoon, I'm off you for life."

"Well, thanks for dropping in," said Coach Brown, "and many thanks for your tip."

Elmer went back to his bench and continued putting on the finishing touches to his dressing.

"What a lot of queer people there are in the world," he thought. "Here is a man who is probably either a successful lawyer, a doctor, business man, salesman, or a barber; like as not he might be unsuccessful in his own line of work, and yet he takes it upon himself to instruct a professional and successful football coach, and to do it just an hour before the big game of the year!"

It was hard for Elmer to understand how Coach Brown held his temper so evenly under all these trying conditions.

But here Elmer's reflections were broken; some one walked over and was standing by his side. He looked up — it was Rip.

"I have a note here from Ruth," said Rip. "She said they all met without any trouble and had lunch together. They'll see us after the game on the mezzanine. Estelle is in the party, and the setting is complete. We're all ready, aren't we, old boy?"

Elmer tried to be nonchalant.

"A football game is just a football game," he began; but inwardly he was glad — glad that Estelle was present with his own people, to watch him make his supreme effort.

Completely dressed Elmer went over to the rosin bag and smeared a quantity of rosin over his jersey, chest, and forearm, and on his pants. Dad Moore smeared a lot of molasses over the front and forearm of the jersey of Berlin, as that young man still had a tendency towards fumbling. This was not necessary in Elmer's case, and he was glad, as the stuff was horribly sticky.

Then — "Everybody out but the players!" called the coach, and the players all arranged themselves in a circle on the floor. The only ones allowed to remain were three old alumni — three successful business men whose hobby was football enthusiasts for the school and the team. They always worked with the coach in every way, and were of invaluable assistance in getting points of view or impressions across to the players. Invariably, they were afraid the team was going to lose and it was because of this gloom complex that the coach always insisted that they be around the team before the game and sit with him on the bench.

With the team now gathered in a circle before him, the coach named the opening line-up — the same line-up that had started the game against Aksarben.

"You're all a little bit too nervous and high strung," he said. "You're too over-anxious, and that means you're going to be off-side a lot; and that means penalties. Let's relax just a little physically, without relaxing mentally. We're going to play a kicking game today, and lay for the breaks. That means we will have to present an impenetrable defense. I'm going to review just a few points that we've been going over during the last few weeks, just to make sure that these ideas are all positively clear in our minds.

"When State uses close formation, I want our ends in there a mile a minute smashing up the formation before it gets a chance to get started. I want the defensive tackles roving around in and out so that the State quarterback can't tell where to expect to find you. I want the defensive guards submarining down underneath, all afternoon, so that the State line can't lift you. But don't play ostrich, or think that for the time being you are a Mohammedan. Never go flat to your stomach. On your second reaction get your head up and have your arms free so that when the man carrying the ball gets near you, you can grab him.

"You defensive center and fullback, you must keep roving around, must keep moving, so the State quarterback can't tell where to find you either. But be at the right place when the ball is snapped. Don't hesitate. Run and analyze at the same time and meet every play with all the punch, force, and determination you can put into it."

He turned next to the defensive halfbacks. "You are responsible mostly for passes," he told them. "Keep talking to each other on defense and keep in contact — know what the other fellow is going to do. Defensive quarterback is responsible for any sneakers, like the shoestring play, where one man will hide out on the sidelines. Every man must be alert every instant, but relax physically whenever you can. Indomitable spirit, irrepressible fight, and an active mind — those are the things that win! No matter what happens, every man must keep saying to himself, 'We Will Win.' I want no one talking to the officials except Captain Ruggles. This is going to be a fierce contest, but I don't want any Dulac man to do anything that isn't fair or within the rules.

"But let's play it hard, boys — there's nothing in the rules against playing the game hard, so hard, in fact, that some of the State boys will begin to think of home, mother, and the sidelines. As the game wears on, you're going to get tired; you're going to be bruised; you're going to feel all in; but that's the time to figure that the boys on the State team feel exactly the same then nothing else counts but guts. Is there anything you want to say, Rip? This is the last game for you, too, Credon, Jones, Higgins, and Kerr."

"Nothing except this," said Rip and his eyes blazed, and his jaw protruded "this is the last game I'll ever play for old Dulac. We've been a lot of pals together all fall, and we've played together, have had a lot of fun together, have studied together, and have fought together. This is the last game for Higgins, Kerr, Credon, and Jones. I know how they feel — they're going out there to give all they have. But how about the rest of you fellows? Are you going out with us, to be one of us, so that regardless of what happens we can hold our heads high and proud?"

"We are," they all chorused; and the heart of every man there contracted with the impact of that promise.

"Then, let's go," said Rip. And the Dulac team stormed out of the door.

As they lined up in the runway of the big stadium, Rip pressed a note into Elmer's hand. On a piece of hotel paper was scrawled in the handwriting of his father, which he knew so well, these words, "Good luck, Mother and Dad." He felt the tears swelling in his eyes; but an instant later he was sprinting in through the gate and on to the gridiron, with his teammates, and everything was forgotten but the game at hand. Up and down the field they went, until the perspiration began to appear on their foreheads. Then to the sidelines, the whole team, except the kickers and receivers.

Jones sent a half dozen kicks soaring fifty to sixty-five yards, down the field. Elmer watched each one of them right into his arms, with never a trace of fumbling or bobbling. His powers of concentration were so intensified that he could not have taken his eyes off the ball if he wanted to. Then he walked over to the sidelines, and sat down beside Coach Brown.

"What's the last word?"

"There's nothing more that I can tell you now, nothing that will be of any help. Meet conditions as they arise, on your own initiative, and if you get behind, don't be discouraged. You have resourcefulness and I have every confidence that you can outwit these other fellows."

Rip came running off the field at this moment. "We've won the toss, and are kicking off." The three shook hands, and out the players went.

Taking the ball from the referee, Elmer held it on the ground with one finger for Jones, who was kicking off.

"Who'll make the first tackle?" called out Captain Rip; and as Elmer glanced around he could see that his ten teammates were like ten race horses, straining at the leash.

"Are you ready, Captain Hughes? Are you ready, Captain Ruggles?"

The referee's whistle sounded, and an instant later Jones sent the ball soaring far over the goal line. The game had actually begun.

Ten Dulac men went sprinting down the field, but Elmer had to stay back as safety. The ball was brought to the twenty yard line, a State player having touched it for a touchback. State lined up in close formation, but Elmer still stayed back, almost forty yards, as he knew that even from close formation his friend Hunk Hughes could punt over fifty yards.

But there were no punts coming. Driving right through the tackles and guards and center, the irresistible golden avalanche from State rolled up the field. Three to five yards a down they came.

"We'll stop them as soon as they get to our thirty yard line," thought Elmer. But there was no stopping them on the thirty yard line. Once Renfrew was held for no gain, but on the next play Hughes plunged right over the Dulac left guard for nine yards, landing squarely on his nose, so terrific had been his forward impetus.

Elmer called the signal which changed the defense to the square formation. He, himself, who was supposed to be back playing safety, found himself up almost on the line of scrimmage, tackling with every ounce of energy that was in him. Still they came on irresistibly pushing the lighter Dulac team before them. Straight to the one yard line — State's ball on the one yard line, first down, four tries to make a touchdown! Elmer called for time out.

The Dulac boys gathered around him in a circle.

Rip had one eye partly closed, his face was so dirty he was almost unrecognizable, and he was sobbing softly. The little one hundred and sixty pound left guard was groggy; already it was apparent that he was all in. The rest of the team were dazed and battered from the terrific storm which had hit them. At that instant out came the only two hundred pounder on the Dulac team, to replace the gallant little left guard who was led to the sidelines, incoherently muttering that "it wasn't fair" — he wanted to be in there "when the ball was kicked off."

"We've got to hold them here or we're licked," said Rip to the other nine teammates, the incoming player being still over to one side, as the rules were quite clear that an incoming substitute was not allowed to communicate with his teammates until one play had elapsed.

"I'll move up to the line of scrimmage," suggested Jones, "making an eight-man line. I'll get between you, Rip, and the tackle. They may not recognize this point, and one of us ought to slip through the line every time."

"Good," said Rip, "let's go back, boys, because if we don't hold them here we're licked — so let's hold them."

The time being up the referee blew his whistle and both teams lined up again.

"We're going to score right through you, Ruggles," said the State quarterback.

"I dare you to," replied the indomitable Rip, as the State quarterback began barking his numbers.

Just before the ball was snapped Jones unobtrusively and unobservedly slipped up to the line between Rip and the tackle. The ball was snapped and the two lines met and for the first time that afternoon the Dulac line, rising to emotional heights, held the giant State line even. But even so, the preponderance of power of the great State backfield must have been such that it would surely have carried them across the goal line, had not Jones slipped through and with his legs well under him met the hard driving Hunk Hughes squarely on the shoulder and tackled him for no gain.

As the two teams scrambled from the ground there was a dazed look in the eyes of the entire State team. Elmer moved up alongside Jones and whispered, "They're watching you now, so you stay back and I'll creep up in your place this time."

At exactly the same spot the State quarterback again sent Hunk Hughes; and this time it was Elmer who slipped through and tackled him for less than six inches gain. Lying under the immense pile, Elmer looked right up into the sweating boyish face of his old friend, Hunk — "Well, you didn't make it that time, old boy."

"Gee whiz, where did you come from?"

A little bit dazed from the shock of the impact, Elmer now lined up back in his usual position. As the State quarterback, looking over the entire Dulac team, was trying to analyze what new angle there was in the Dulac defense, Elmer walked over and patted Jones on the back, and as he did so, he turned his head and whispered back to Credon, "It's your turn to go up on the line between the left guard and tackle."

Once more the trick worked, the guess was correct; the State quarter this time sent Renfrew plunging through the opposite side of the line, only to be met by Credon just before he got to the line of scrimmage. It was fourth down, and still one yard to go. As they were lining up, Elmer whispered into the ears of Miller, Jones, and Credon, "Look out for a forward pass this time, boys; we'll have to stay back."

The morale of the Dulac line had risen one hundred per cent. in the last three downs, and on the next play they stopped Renfrew without gain, mainly, however, because the State quarterback made the mistake of shooting the play directly at Rip. The Dulac team had held them for four downs when it seemed an impossibility. It was now their ball.

"Punt formation," called Elmer, and as Jones went back in the kicking position Elmer took his place as the second man in the tandem on the right. State played their center over to the strong side and their fullback came over to the weak side. Elmer had an impulse to call for a plunge through center, or for a forward pass; however, he stifled the impulse as he realized that their entire safety here depended on a long kick up the field.

"Ends in tight," he called and the two ends, who were out wide, lined up close to the tackles so as to help them keep out the fullback and the center who were trying to crash in the flanks. As Elmer was calling the signals, he sauntered back towards Jones.

"Jonesey, old boy, you'll have to kick it out of bounds." Faultlessly the center passed the ball back to Jones, and, as Elmer picked himself off the ground after having blocked the big tackle coming through, he found that Jones had sent a wonderful punt down the field, which rolled out of bounds after having traveled sixty-six yards.

"Well, that wins the game for us," said Rip to his teammates as they were lined up on defense. "Now let's take the ball away from them, and we'll march for a touchdown."

But his prediction was not true. Stung to the quick by the unexpected resistance offered at the goal line, the State team now began
to hit, if anything, even harder than before. Straight down the field
they came for a second march. No deception — no doubt as to who
had the ball or where he was going, as the quarterback headed every play. It was simply irresistible power. Three and five yards at a
down they came, straight to the eight yard line.

At this point Hunk Hughes went crashing off tackle and though
both Credon and Elmer tackled him, he had so powerful a leg drive
that he shook them both off and rolled across the goal line clear for
the first touchdown.

Elmer felt his heart sink as they lined up between the goal posts,
while the State team was making its effort to score the extra point.

"At this rate," he thought, "they will beat us twenty-eight or thirty
points. My, what a team!"

Renfrew place kicked the ball squarely between the goal posts
and the score stood seven to nothing.

"What shall I do?" asked Rip of Elmer.

"Kick off to them," said Elmer. "If they can march eighty yards
against us again, we can't beat them no matter what we do. Our
only hope lies in letting them have the ball and tiring themselves
out."

Again Jones kicked the ball across the goal line, but an instant
after he had done so the official time-keeper announced the end of
the quarter and both teams changed goals. Now the State team
started up the field, five and six yards at a try, reaching Dulac's forty
yard line before the first break of the game occurred. Renfrew
fumbled, and like a flash, Kerr, Dulac's left end, pounced on it. It
was a lucky break for Dulac, as her morale was in suspense.

"If they had marched for one more touchdown," thought Elmer,
"there's no telling how many they would have romped on to during
the rest of the game."

On the first play, Elmer called Credon off-tackle, but he failed to
gain. Elmer then tried the other side, and found that State's right
tackle was just as relentless a driver, and Miller lost a yard — making it third down. He heard Hunk Hughes warning his teammates

about the forward pass, so he lined up on punt formation and called for a punt. Standing on his own thirty yard line, Jones got away a beautiful punt which rolled out of bounds on the fifteen yard line. Elmer again blocked the big tackle who was coming through trying to block the punt, and this time he felt a twinge of pain in his side as he charged into the big hulk of humanity which was on its way to the kicker. However, he felt no after effects, but got up, and jogging down the field, slapped Jones on the back.

"That's the greatest kicking you've ever done in your life, old boy! If we can get a few breaks, we'll win this game yet."

The State team kicked on first down and as Elmer caught the punt in midfield, despite the fact that he was thrown heavily to the ground by the State end, he laughed to himself. He would win; he would be victorious; he knew what he would do.

From his present advantageous position he could keep running two plays, and with Jones kicking as well as he was, he would keep State in a hole the remaining half. Then in the second half he would open up with his passes and there was still a chance that they could show up well. And this was just exactly what happened. For some reason State now played a kicking game. Elmer would run off two plays as slowly as he could, and then on third down Jones would punt it back to State again. The half ended with the ball in Dulac's possession in the middle of the field. As Elmer sat down in the dressing room between the halves he felt that same twinge of pain in his side again, but it was gone in an instant.

For seven or eight minutes the entire Dulac team, tired, battered, and bruised, lay at full length, resting up for the next half.

Coach Brown came over and knelt down beside Elmer. "Our only chance is to forward pass as soon as we get the ball next half, Elmer, because if State starts that offense of theirs again they'll simply push us off the field. Coach Smith will probably tell his quarterback to do this and I don't believe you'll find them making the mistake this next half of playing the kicking game with us. So take a chance; throw a flock of forward passes. They are our only hope."

As the State captain had the choice at the start of the second half, he chose to receive.

"Gosh, if they march for a touchdown," thought Elmer, "it's all off with us. We'll have to play for a break."

Now almost entirely recuperated, and full of fresh vim and vigor, the Dulac team lined up, talking it up, and full of aggressive spirit. For the third time that day, Jones on the kickoff, sent the ball far over the goal line. "Well, they have eighty yards to go," thought Elmer to himself, "and it's a long way."

Starting on her own twenty yard line, again the State team moved up the field, at a pace and with a power that made the Dulac line seem helpless to resist them. As they got to midfield, however, again Dulac got a break. With second down, five yards to go, Hunk Hughes started for the line and stumbled; before he could recover his feet he was downed by three or four blue-jerseyed athletes. "Third down, seven," announced the referee.

"Move up close," whispered Elmer to all the backs, "but be alert for the forward pass which is sure to come as a result."

The State quarterback pondered for an instant — saw how close all the Dulac backs were and began calling his numbers.

"Signals," Hunk Hughes sang out, — again the State quarterback gave his numbers; and once more Hunk bellowed, "signals!"

They wrangled for an instant; then, as the State quarterback repeated his numbers there was no interruption. Straight back to Hunk Hughes came the ball, and Hunk faded back and to one side. Elmer saw that the State left end had got by Miller and was streaking towards him. Elmer was dropping back to cover him, as he saw the ball launched into the air. He relaxed and coiled himself, and at just the right time he jumped as high into the air as he could, though he could feel the body of the State end bump alongside him. Extending himself to the utmost, Elmer felt the ball hit his fingers, and he pushed it as hard as he could to one side. The next instant he was lying flat on his back with the State end on top of him.

The wind was entirely knocked out of him. It was a queer sensation. Rip called for time and Dad Moore ran out from the sidelines, thumped him on the back a few times, wiped his face, and Elmer felt himself again.

"Dulac's ball, first down," announced the referee, waving his arms towards Dulac's goal.

"What happened?" asked Elmer, turning to his teammates.

"Why, you knocked the ball right into my arms," said Miller, "so it's our ball."

"Another break in our favor," thought Elmer; and taking stock of the situation, he saw that they had the ball on their own twenty-five yard line.

"49, 57, 18, 42," — they shifted to the right, Elmer took the ball from center, and made as if he were giving it to Jones, who plunged right into the line. But Elmer had not given the ball to Jones, he still held it himself, and taking several steps back until he was sure he was five yards behind the line of scrimmage, he turned and whipped the ball straight up the middle of the field, right into the arms of Kerr, the left end, who had run in behind Renfrew. Renfrew had been sucked up into the line, and Kerr would have gone for a long gain, but for a spectacular tackle by Hunk Hughes. Jones was hurt in the play and time was taken out. The injury proved to be only a painful wrench of the ankle, which caused Jones to limp during the rest of the game.

The ball was now in midfield; the first play had gained thirty yards. "What to play?"

"Never mind about any line plunges," Elmer heard Hunk Hughes call to Renfrew. "Our line can stop them. Lay back, Renfrew, for passes."

So on the next play Elmer shot Jones into the line. Two yards was the best that Jones could gain, and next he called on Credon to run tackle. There was no gain on this play, so Elmer tried a trick play which was smothered by the hard charging State line. "Fourth down, ten," announced the referee.

"I'm afraid you'll have to punt," said Jones. "I can run on my ankle, but I'm afraid I can't kick at all with it."

So they lined up on punt formation, with Elmer back in the kicker's position.

Elmer was now standing on his own forty yard line. He ran over in his mind quickly the various angles to the situation. He could punt forty yards only, which would mean that State would get the ball on about their twenty or twenty-five yard line, and then, of course, State would come back again with that same offensive. The light Dulac line were not superhuman, and the chances were that they would go to pieces any minute, beaten right into the ground.

Quickly he made his decision, called his numbers, and the next instant found the ball in his arms. Going through all the preliminary motions of a punt, he stopped just before the completion, checked the ball, and whirled it straight into the arms of Miller, the halfback, just beyond the line of scrimmage.

Thirty yards up the field was Hunk Hughes, thinking a punt was coming and as a result chasing and trying to block the Dulac right end. He had been caught entirely napping. Down the field like a flash went Miller, and with a beautiful sidestep he swept by Hughes, and Elmer, coming up the field, could see all the disappointment and surprise in Hunk's face as he sprawled on the ground clutching frantically at the empty air. The Dulac right end interfered with the State quarterback just enough so that Miller outsprinted him for the goal line.

It was a touchdown! — Dulac's first touchdown!

There was exultation in Elmer's heart, and his feet, which the minute previous had been heavy and leaden, were now light and full of spring.

Dulac lined up on the five yard line to make their extra point. "You'd better try it yourself," said Jones. "My ankle is getting weaker every minute"; and so with Jones holding the ball, Elmer essayed the place kick. His leg, however, instead of inscribing the vertical arc, had a little lateral motion to it and the ball swung to one side of the posts. Elmer was so outraged he was helpless. The score board read State seven, Dulac six. The loud cheering in the Dulac sections had died down, and there was renewed activity in the State sections.

The State captain elected to kickoff. Elmer felt himself growing moody and despondent as he walked back to receive the kickoff. "Here I had the chance to tie the score and missed it! Here I had the chance — just a measly little place kick, and I botched it!" He berated himself unmercifully as he looked over toward the sidelines, and there, as clear as a photograph, he could see the face of Coach Smith looking out his way, and laughing uproariously. Instantly all the despondency and gloom was gone — in its place came a flame of vigor and determination. He fought with himself to stay cool and found it difficult.

Renfrew kicked off for State, and failing to be accurate, the ball curved to the left and was caught by Kerr, Dulac's left end. Without hesitation, Kerr started forward, and covered ten yards before he was downed on the thirty-five yard line.

Elmer called his numbers and shifted to the right, the same play that he had tried earlier so successfully, a fake line plunge, followed by a pass to Kerr. But this time it failed to work. Renfrew covered Kerr and almost intercepted the pass.

First an end run, and then a trick play failed to gain; so Elmer decided to drop back and punt. He punted forty yards. The State quarterback was tackled in his tracks by Kerr, who was playing the game of his life.

To his surprise, Elmer now saw State introduce the complex part of its offense — double passes, triple passes, spinner plays. Yet, for some reason or other, this stuff failed to work. The Dulac team watched the quarterback closely; it seemed impossible for the State team to get going again. After several exchanges of kicks in the fourth quarter, State even tried the fake reverse play. Even that failed to gain. The fire seemed to have gone out of State's offense, and as the game drew towards a close it was evident to Elmer that Dulac's opponents were already becoming satisfied with their one point margin.

In desperation, Elmer, when Dulac had the ball, tried one or two long passes, fifty yards in length, but these were either incomplete or intercepted. Standing on his own forty yard line, first down, ten, Elmer was perplexed as to what to try. The line was still in there, doggedly doing the best they could. He turned around and looked at his own backfield; but only Credon was in any shape to do himself justice. Jones' ankle was paining so badly that he could hardly run at all. Miller had absorbed an awful lot of punishment, and there was a dazed look in his eyes — he was out there, but that was about all. There was no use calling on Credon to carry the ball, since neither Miller nor Jones were able to furnish any interference. The kicking game would get him nowhere. The forward passing game was not the thing, as State's backfield men were lying back waiting for them. State's ends, who in the first part of the game had been playing rather wide, were now playing closely, and smashing. Elmer determined to use himself.

He called the numbers; they shifted to the right. He took the ball from center and gave it to Jones, who plunged into the line for no gain. Again Elmer called out his numbers; they shifted to the right again; and once more Elmer, the same as before, apparently gave the ball to Jones — but in actuality, hid it for an instant, then went sprinting around the State end who had been sucked in.

A new flash of exultation swept through Elmer's breast, but it was short lived. The next instant something hit him, and he was down with a dull thud.

Looking up, he saw the face of his old friend, Hunk. It was Hunk who had spoiled the run. The joy of victory was in Hunk's eyes.

"I hated to do it, Elmer, but we've got to win this game," he said as he got up.

As Elmer stood to his feet he found that he ached in every joint. He suddenly felt tired, — listless; what was the use? State had too good a team and Dulac had already made a far better showing than her friends had any right to expect.

He turned to the referee. "How much time left to play?"

"A minute and thirty seconds."

"Punt formation," called Elmer.

He was close to the side where the State bench was situated. As he stood back in kicker's position his eyes rolled over to the bench and to his surprise and anger, he saw Coach Smith with his hand cupped, calling out to his backfield men. It must have been that the referee looked over at exactly the same time, because he instantly walked up and picking up the ball, announced. "Fifteen yards, penalty. Coach Smith coaching from the side line." And picking up the ball he carried it fifteen yards, which placed the ball on State's forty-five yard line.

Out on the field came the furious Smith. He was so enraged that his face was livid. Up to the referee he came, shaking his finger.

"What are you trying to do, give Dulac the game? Why don't you make them earn what they get?"

"Fifteen more yards for coming on the field without permission," said the referee.

"This is the last time you'll ever work in a State game," bellowed Smith. "I'll make it so hot you'll never get any games refereeing around this part of the country again."

"If you don't get off the field real quick, and keep quiet, I'll make it fifteen more," said the referee, apparently unperturbed. Smith stopped talking at once and sullenly made his way back to the sidelines.

The ball now rested on State's thirty-yard line though quite a bit over toward the sidelines. "Call on everything you have," whispered Elmer to Miller, "and try to get tackled in the middle of the field. I want to try a place kick on the next play."

Drawing on all his reserve strength, Miller sprinted around the end, and though he gained only a yard he had put the ball in fine position for a place kick.

"Well, Jonesey, I'll put it up to you. Don't you think, you can take that leg of yours and forget about your bad ankle for just about two or three seconds?"

"I wish I could," said Jones, "but it's absolutely impossible. I'll hold the ball, and you kick it."

Just then Elmer heard a voice: "Referee, I'm taking Jones' place at fullback," and turning around he recognized Berlin.

With tears streaming down his cheeks, Jones hobbled off the field, carrying with him the congratulations of his teammates.

Leaning down, exactly on State's forty yard line, Elmer signaled Berlin back to the kicker's position. They were in place kick formation. Just at that instant out came a substitute from the State bench who replaced Renfrew at fullback.

"What was that for, I wonder?" said Elmer to himself. "It's fourth down, ten — about all we can do is kick."

And as the referee blew his whistle announcing that play might start, Elmer began calling numbers denoting a kick. But as he did so, he noticed the State fullback sneak up on to the line between the guard and tackle on his left side.

Quick as a flash Elmer weighed the facts. A forty yard place kick was too far for Berlin. He was only accurate on short place kicks inside the twenty-five yard line.

Elmer kept on calling out numbers, and the whole team was quivering, waiting for the snap signal, when suddenly, he interjected the check number — thirty-three. This check number, thirty-three, meant that all numbers called previously were null and void and that new numbers denoting a new play were forthcoming.

There was not a sign on Elmer's face that he had seen anything or that there had been any change in his plans. Quickly he called the numbers, "45, 54, 69." Back came the ball, but before it reached him Elmer had risen up and catching it cleanly, dropped back into the right, several yards. The State left end changed his course, stopped, and stood still until it was too late — he was evidently expecting Elmer to try to run around him.

Throwing the ball straight over his shoulder Elmer sailed a bullet-like pass right into the arms of Miller, who, after a short delay had run right into the territory vacated by the new defensive fullback. With the ease and grace of an outfielder in the big leagues, Miller got the ball, sidestepped the State quarterback, and was over the goal line.

Elmer could hardly believe it. He had acted more on impulse than anything else. He could still hardly believe it was true, even when Credon kicked the extra point, and the score board read, Dulac thirteen, State seven. Dulac was ahead!

State elected to receive and Elmer himself, kicking off, purposely kicked short so that time would be consumed. Sure enough, just as the State tackle who received the kickoff was downed, there came a sharp crack of the referee's pistol, and the next instant the crowd was all over the field.

Dulac had won! Dulac had beaten State!

Fighting himself clear from some delirious Dulac rooters who insisted on carrying him on their shoulders, Elmer worked himself to one side and finally got to the dressing room. There, through a strange coincidence, the very first player he met was Hunk Hughes. The two old chums rushed together to shake hands. No game or contest could come between their friendship.

"Well, we beat you," said Elmer, "but you sure had the better team."

"Oh, I don't know about that," said Hunk, "but I want to congratulate you. You certainly think too quickly for us. And I guess you're right about Coach Smith — I want to apologize for his actions this afternoon."

"No apologies necessary," Elmer laughed. "He won the game for us!"

I've got to congratulate you, Elmer. on the fine team you've got — a wonderful bunch of boys."

"The same to you — and say, Hunk, I'll see you up at the hotel this evening, won't I?"

After his shower bath, as Elmer was putting on his street clothes he was surprised to feel no particular spirit of exultation, after all his years of preparation for this greatest event of his life. True, he found a certain sense of satisfaction in the victory; but that was all. He felt sorry for the State team and for Hunk Hughes, his old friend; and he even felt sorry for Coach Smith. He began to see things more at their true value; he began to realize that a football game is just a football game, and not a thing of vital importance after all. He found that what he imagined was hatred for Coach Smith had been purely boyish emotion, and that it had grown simply because he had made no attempt to check it. He realized now that he no longer hated Coach Smith, — the idea was absurd! — and that so far as average human beings go, Coach Smith, after all, was not such a bad fellow. He was a man with certain frailties — but no one is perfect.

As Elmer and Rip walked up the street toward the hotel a few minutes later, there was no gloating or "crowing" in their hearts; even the exhilaration which had carried them through the game, was gone. A comfortable sense of satisfaction, that comes from duty well done, of a task well performed — this was the sum total of the boys' feelings.

As Elmer sat at the dinner table a little later in the evening he relaxed and felt happy, quietly happy in a new and restful way. He felt happy because of his parents, who seemed to take such a keen pride in his achievements; because of the good friends he had made, worthwhile friends; because those in whom he was most interested were sitting around the same table with him now, happy with him.

His parents were there, Estelle was there, and Ruth, Ruth's mother, and Rip's father and mother, old Professor Noon — they were all there. The crowd was a jolly one, in an extremely joyous mood. But to Elmer Estelle seemed shy and a little remote, a little far away. Where the others in their congratulations had been profuse, she had been very brief and rather detached. Only once during the course of the dinner did he catch her eye. She smiled sweetly, then, but Elmer couldn't quite tell whether it was a smile for himself or for his mother who sat next to him.

There was a lull in the conversation while they were waiting for their coffee.

"Well, now that you have achieved your ambition in athletics, my dear Elmer," said Professor Noon, "and with your scholastic work of such a caliber that I believe I can safely say you will be graduated in June, what new worlds are you going out to conquer? Come, speak up a bit; you've been too quiet and reserved down there all evening."

"I'm just tired out, I guess," Elmer answered; "so I hope you'll pardon my quietness this evening. But I have a little good news that I know will interest you. I had a talk just before dinner with Coach Brown and his friend, Judge Sommers — you know he's the biggest lawyer in town; and what do you think? — this summer I can go into the Judge's law office to take a position which I hope will be permanent. And more than that, Coach Brown has seen the authorities at Dulac and has carte blanche to offer me a position as assistant coach next fall at a good salary. The coaching work won't interfere with my law work in any way."

Here Elmer's father spoke up. "Yes," he said, "it's all true — and of course Elmer's mother and I are glad, especially about the chance to go with Judge Sommers. But," he smiled, "we're not quite so sure of the coaching work. But Elmer has already done things so well, we're willing to let him decide."

"I am not going into coaching as a profession," Elmer explained to the company. "Coach Brown tells me it is the worst profession one can go into. He says you can't tell from one year to another where you stand. The papers write a lot of exaggerated tales about coaches' salaries, but these stories are generally stretched out of all proportion to truth. A good, average successful practitioner of law would turn up his nose at the salary paid the highest salaried coach in America.

"But I do like football, and I hope I can help Coach Brown for two or three seasons. The salary I get will come in very handy; the average young lawyer doesn't make very much the first few years. Ask Dad!"

They all laughed heartily at this, and Mr. Higgins laughed loudest and longest.

"You're right there, Elmer," he said. "I had to practice law eight years before I was financially able to marry your mother."

"There goes the orchestra," said Rip. "Let's go up and dance a few dances; our train doesn't leave for an hour and a half yet."

So excusing themselves the young folks made their way out. Up on the mezzanine floor Elmer motioned Estelle over to one side, away from the crowd. The strains of the orchestra came faintly to their ears as they sat there several minutes quietly, without saying a word.

"There's an awful jam in there," said Elmer at last, "and I hope you don't mind if I'm tired and prefer sitting here."

Estelle smiled. "That's just the way I feel, too."

"That's fine," said Elmer, "you always seem to understand. Besides there'd be an endless crowd wanting to shake hands and ask questions. I'd much rather sit here with you."

There was another silence; then Elmer spoke again.

"I'm going back to Dulac to practice law, and I'm going to make enough being assistant coach so that I think I can save some money — but most of all I am going to be back at Dulac — what do you think?"

"I think," said Estelle, as his fingers closed over hers, "I think it's wonderful."

The end of *The Four Winners.*

Printed in the United States
20397LVS00003B/1-81

9 780972 982108